MOTHER'S DAY

A COLLECTION OF SHORT STORIES

VIRGINIA GWYNN

MOTHER'S DAY

The stories within this book are either fictionalized versions of past events or are purely products of the author's imagination, in which case any similarities to actual persons, living or deceased, names, characterizations, recorded events, or incidents are unintentional.

First Publication Date: April 2014

ISBN: 978-1497381490

Published by Southern Star Press, LLC

SOUTHERN STAR PRESS
An Independent Publisher

Cover Design by Charity Myers
www.thecreativepooldesign.com

Printed in the United States of America

MOTHER'S DAY

For

Mama
And
Lynnie

ACKNOWLEDGEMENTS

I especially appreciate the friendship and support of the long-time Wednesday Night Writers, Richard Dempsey, Gina Edwards, Adrian Fogelin, Leslee Horner, Leigh Muller and Linda Sturgeon, who have pushed and pulled and laughed and cried with me for more years than I can recall. They may well know some of my stories by heart!

I am grateful to my loving friends in The Last Word Book Club whose interest in good books and conversation has inspired me for over fifty years.

I am fortunate that my content editor, author Adrian Fogelin (slow-dancejournal.wordpress.com), and my line editor, Gina Edwards (AroundTheWritersTable.com), were both good at their jobs and cheerleaders to boot. And I was lucky to have the help of a great reader and useful critic, C.S. Faris, and my special readers, Susan Baumler and Sarah Ann Dailey.

Author Donna Meredith (DonnaMeredith.com) worked her magic in getting the manuscript ready for the printer and Charity Myers (thecreativepooldesign.com) read my mind when she designed the Mother's Day cover.

The interest of the teachers, professors, and other writers who took the time to notice and nurture my first writing efforts was invaluable.

Thank you one and all.

To my children, Lina, Jimmy, and David, who have always believed that what I write is worth reading, and who make my life worth living, my eternal love and gratitude.

To Mary Lina, Sara Clifton, Isabelle, Susanna, Meghan, Lina Blake, Clifton Elizabeth, Zack, George, and Clifton, magnificent bright lights in my life, I love you dearly.

And to my daddy, who introduced me to short stories when I was a young girl and inspired me to create those of my own, I wish you were here with me now.

MOTHER'S DAY

Sometimes I feel like a motherless child.
                    - Old Negro Spiritual

THE COCA COLA KID

When I was growing up in Atlanta, the hometown of Coca Cola, we lived in an area near Buckhead with large homes lining tree-shaded streets. While our smaller cottage was torn down for reasons which escape me now, my grandmother's house still stands. Except for the growth of the shrubs and trees, it looks pretty much the way it did when we went to live with Granny during the war.

Daddy was in the Army Air Corps, stationed at a beachfront camp down in Florida. He wrote again and again that he expected to be shipped out at any time. He thought, that for Mama and William and me, to move in with Granny Howard was the best plan. He did not want us living alone, he said. To please him, we packed and moved three blocks to the house where Mama was raised.

So while Daddy trained on a sandy airstrip in the Sunshine State, and later when he had been shipped out to England and was flying P51 night missions, Mama and her friends sat on Granny's front porch and drank what Granny referred to as "the nectar of the Southern gods."

Morning, afternoon, and early evening, they drank Coca Colas. While rumors continue that the first recipe for this marvelously addictive Southern concoction contained extract from the coca plant, we all became addicted much later, when the sugar, caffeine, taste, and fizz were enough to do the trick.

Granny Howard was born and raised in Atlanta before it was

such an overwhelming city. She grew up during a time of grace and manners, and she did her best to pass along the need to uphold these conventions even, or perhaps especially, during a time of war.

She was not alone in this. Civilized women at home were expected to carry on as best they could in a mostly female society, doing what was possible to help their fighting men and women, but not neglecting—even with the rationing of gas, butter, sugar, and meat—the small important gatherings for food and friendship. Friends gladly shared ration coupons to make it possible.

In the summer of '42, Mama and Granny hosted two Coke parties. During that summer after second grade, I was allowed to help by passing a silver tray of little tomato and cucumber sandwiches and the pimiento cheese triangles made with just a smidgeon of onion.

After Labor Day, when white shoes had been returned to their closets to hibernate and we children had returned to the public school system and someone else's care, they held the first of their Wednesday morning bridge parties. To round out two tables, six guests were invited for ten o'clock. The menu changed and tiny biscuits with potted ham spread and egg and olive tea sandwiches were served as accompaniment for the luncheons of tomato aspic or molded chicken salad.

Occasionally, there was rice pudding or tapioca with canned fruit cocktail for dessert. In winter, if there was sugar to spare, Granny would make her delicious gingerbread with lemon sauce. Always, salted peanuts were put out for anyone who wished to lace her Coke.

I looked forward to these Wednesdays with as much enthusiasm as any of the guests. I could count on Mama to leave me a small china plate of the leftovers in the ice box with a note that said "FOR NELL – DO NOT TOUCH!" It was our little joke. William would *never* have touched such "sissy food." He was two years older and had no interest in party food. He preferred light bread spread with Oleo that we color-mixed ourselves, sprinkled with sugar.

William did his best to escape the front porch where the ladies gathered in the warmer months or the front parlor rooms where they met and gossiped on cold days. My brother spent his free time in his room, making model airplanes or playing war with his buddies in one backyard or another. On Saturday mornings, I was allowed to join them in the European trenches or the jungles of Burma. William was always a flyboy in the RAF. He bunked in a makeshift Quonset hut, just like Daddy.

We fashioned a hospital under the draping limbs of the mimosas by the back fence. I wore my dime store Red Cross nurse's outfit and carried my brown leather shoulder bag while I bandaged serious wounds and wiped feverish brows. All the while, I served up small tin teacups of nourishing co' cola to the injured boys. The terminal cases were allowed a single colored sugar pill and a sip of water. No need to waste a Coke on the dying.

Every other Wednesday morning when there was no bridge game, Mama and two of her best friends went to St. Luke's to pack boxes for overseas and to sort garments for The Clothes Closet. After their three-hour shift, they walked home by way of the Chat 'n' Nibble Tearoom, stopping in to have the day's special. The small restaurant was famous locally for its vegetable soup served with tiny sizzling corn cakes. Mama took along a Mason jar to fill with soup to bring home for our supper. She served it with William's favorite, a grilled Spam sandwich which I couldn't stand, so I ate Oysterettes.

Granny said her house had been lonesome since Grandpa died before I was born, but then we came to live with her and that made all the difference. Living there, with Daddy away, all I knew for those growing up years was the company of women. We had Sam who kept the yard mowed and raked and Mr. Bascomb at the A&P, our Negro ice man, and the milkman with a badly turned foot who wasn't drafted and couldn't enlist, and there were others, so William and I did have contact with men. But that was different.

Sometimes I wondered what it might be like to have a full-time father. I never believed my life would have been any better for it.

Mama wrote to Daddy nearly every day. William and I were required to write once a week. At first after Daddy left, I meant every word of what I wrote when I said I missed him and wished he'd come home soon. He was the only one who would play Chinese checkers with me. And he would walk us up to Hildreath's Drugs for ice cream after supper on Fridays. I missed the smell of his Old Spice. William said he missed Daddy so much that he would write to President Roosevelt if he thought it would do any good. Later, I felt guilty because saying I missed him was no longer true.

If anything, I thought having Daddy at home might change the routine, keep us from having our frequent tea parties. He might object to our daily porch visits where I sat to the side, listening and learning as the women talked and gossiped, some wrapping rolls of gauze bandages while others learned to knit under Granny's supervision. He would have surely objected to the noise when we had to move inside because of the weather.

No, it was better this way.

It was on Granny's porch where I heard that her best friend's son had lost his leg in France and was going to be fitted with a wooden one with a painted shoe. I asked if it would be red, like the one on my Raggedy Andy. "No, honey, it will be black, I'm sure," Mama said.

"Well, I guess he'll never be able to wear a brown suit . . . and his real shoe will have to match the painted one or it will look funny."

"I suppose you're right, Nell," Mama said, as she held up her knitting to count stitches.

On the same porch, I saw Sarah Anne Jones weep into Mama's lap because her husband, a corporal in General Patton's Army, had gone missing. I was sitting on the steps playing jacks when, several weeks later, she came running down the street and up our front walk, waving a telegram. Mama held her again, but this time, there were tears of joy.

The porch is where I learned that nylon stockings were a premium gift, that nothing beat getting a letter from the man you love, and that everyone who came onto that porch was concerned about someone in a far off place. I first saw a newborn baby being rocked on our porch and I took a peek at him being nursed, still one of the most erotic things I have ever seen. I had seen movies with combat scenes which gave me bad dreams, but on the porch I heard tales of bravery and honor about men whose lives touched our own. Mr. Brinson, our old butcher, had pushed his partner out of the line of fire and "taken a bullet to his leg." Mrs. Cullom's older son, John, was a captain who "led his platoon to safety during a terrible siege."

I witnessed what it was to be a woman, to stand by your husband, your fiancé, your boyfriend, no matter the circumstances, no matter how frightened or lonely you might be. And I learned the importance of having women friends.

I watched those women help each other, grieve with each other, celebrate and share their lives like family. They also taught me what it meant to be loyal, and when Mona Jolley, whose husband was "over there," took up with "that 4F Swinson man," I learned firsthand what it meant to be disgraced.

It was at Granny's that William and I heard the adults talking one cold Sunday morning about the bombing of a far off island called Pearl Harbor, not realizing at the time that this event would change our world forever. It was also there where we celebrated VE Day. Granny's house was full of neighbors cheering the end of the war. William and I got to stay up past midnight. From our porch, we could hear car horns and bells and sirens in every direction and all the lights came on. No more blackout curtains.

Mama and William and I had waved from Granny's porch as a Checker cab carried Daddy off to war. We were standing on those same steps to see his taxi pull up again nearly four years later.

And, just as she and Granny had done for all their friends and visitors who had come and gone through the house over those thirty-odd months, as soon as Daddy hugged us all and settled into the swing with William and me on either side, Mama slipped into the kitchen and came back to surprise Daddy with a welcome home dish of salted peanuts and an ice cold bottle of Coke.

The Inheritance

According to Mama, nothing says summer like her home-grown tomatoes, warm from the garden, red and ripe, peeled and sliced, sprinkled with salt and pepper, lying smothered with homemade mayonnaise between two soft slices of Sunbeam bread. Mama values this warm weather treat above watermelon and hand-churned fresh peach ice cream. Now, that's saying a lot.

Up until I was about ten years old, Mama bought her summer tomatoes and white sweet corn from Mr. Sweeney's farm stand. Once every week, more often if we had company, we'd make a vegetable run out to the Sweeney's farm. I loved the smell of the fertilizer and newly turned earth mixed with the odor of chemical spray used to ward off gnawing insects and nasty little worms. Knowing what I do today, sniffing that spray and the gas fumes at the service station is probably what killed brain cells and has made me so forgetful.

When the stand was open on Saturdays, Mr. Sweeney took the money, carefully counting out change from a large, worn leather pouch attached to his belt by a metal chain. His weathered hands and the purse were very nearly the same color. While he bagged our produce and made change, his wife and daughter worked their magic, filling cardboard containers with pint after pint of crowder peas, baby and speckled limas, black eyes, purple hulls, and the tiny delicate ladyfingers.

Mrs. Sweeney and their daughter, Belinda, sat next to each

other in old wood-frame farm chairs, the seat slats woven from cured deer hide. They pulled up their generous aprons at the edges so as not to lose any of the precious peas they hulled or beans they snapped that might fail to fall into the rust-spotted blue metal pans resting in their ample laps.

Mama visited with Mr. Sweeney, distracting him while she checked the corn silk for worms and felt the just-picked tomatoes, looking for the best. She would nod and smile in the direction of the heavy, finely mustached Mrs. Sweeney and her near-twin, less-than-bright daughter. Neither woman ever gave more than a nod. I never heard either utter a word. I stood by, mesmerized by what they could do with such monotonous ease.

The summer I turned eleven, Mama suddenly decided to grow tomatoes of her own. She began with one small tray of plants cultivated from seeds she had saved from the year before.

That first season, her plants were started in pots, staked with bamboo slats, tied with strips of her nylons, and set out on the back porch where they caught the sun for most of the day. We continued to drive out to the Sweeney's for vegetables, but Mama never bought another tomato, always relying on her own little crop to supply our table. I asked why she had decided to grow tomatoes, wasn't it a lot of trouble?

"It's a long story, honey. I'll tell you one day."

I'd forgotten about the tomato growing until Mama appeared on my doorstep early this March with a brown envelope in hand. I was at home with four-year-old Annie when she stopped by. Inside the envelope was a list and a small packet of dried tomato seeds from last season.

"It's time for you to plant tomatoes, Betsy, and I'm here to get you started. Get what's on this list and I'll be back next week to help you get it done."

"Why on earth would I want to plant tomatoes?" I asked. She waved away my question as she left.

"Trust me. Next week. I'll tell you then."

I did as she said, if for no other reason than to get an answer to my question. The list read: three clay pots (not too small) and stakes, potting soil and a trowel, liquid fertilizer (preferably Miracle Gro), and a small watering can. It was probably ten days before Mama came around again. I was irritated and anxious to know what this was all about. After the seeds were planted and watered and the pots set on the sun porch window ledge to catch the best sun of the day, Mama said, "Now, after we wash up, I'll tell you about the tomato planting while you fix us a cup of tea."

I set out cups and sliced a lemon. We sat at the kitchen table so that I could watch Annie through the window as she played in the fenced-in side yard.

"You know that I never knew my father, that he died before I was born and Mother never spoke of him," Mama began. I nodded, wondering where this story was headed. "Well, the summer you were ten, when I was thirty, I found out something altogether different. Your grandfather, it seemed, was alive and not so very well, living an hour from us, in a tiny house where he had lived since before he met my mother."

"Good Lord," I said. "What in the world?"

"It was that ridiculous old story—the girl from the good family, falling in love with the boy from the wrong side of the tracks. In this case, my father was some twelve years older, which made keeping them apart even more imperative as far as Mother's folks were concerned."

I searched her face for clues. How must she feel now, telling me this; how did she feel then, when she heard that news?

"Wow!" I said, standing up. I took another look at Annie who was earnestly digging in her sand pile. I turned up the heat under the kettle. "So, then what?"

"Well, Mother said she was sent away to stay with friends in Arizona for two years. The story when she came back was that she had been in school there, met and married a darling guy, Charlie Wilson—this, to give her a married name—who accidentally drowned before he even knew she was pregnant. A sad tale, guaranteed to elicit sympathy and not too many questions. Mother had to promise she'd never let me know my father, that she'd never see him again. That was the caveat to an agreement that her parents would offer their home and support to us. As far as I could tell, they had all kept the agreement."

Mama seemed a little nervous, hesitating from time to time. It was so personal, I felt as if I had invaded her privacy. It was hard to know how to respond.

"Mother did say that a time or two over the years, my father called to check on me.

Once, when I was seven, she sent him my school picture. But they never saw each other again. And neither of them ever married."

I took the kettle off the burner. "That's so sad." I held out my hand and Mama passed me her cup. I poured scalding water over a fresh teabag and offered her the saucer of sliced lemons.

Hearing the story of her missing father, I wondered what it must have been like to discover that a major part of her childhood wasn't true. "And poor Grandmother, having to live a lie all those years—and losing her love." It seemed too archaic to be true. "So, did you ever see your father? And by the way, what does all this have to do with the tomatoes?"

"Ah," she said, "the tomatoes. Well, after Mother told me, I decided I wanted to meet my daddy. Mother said she wasn't certain it was a good idea, but she understood. She gave me his name and address. He lived in a small town some fifty miles away. Even if it was to be just the one time, I knew I had to see him. I got his number from information and made the call.

"My hands shook and I thought I might faint, but I did it. I introduced myself and there was a short silence while it sank in. 'My, my,' he kept saying. 'Imagine that.' I asked if I might come to meet him. 'That would be fine,' he said. And so, a few days later, standing on the front steps of his cinderblock house, I was face to face with the man who, until a few days before, had never existed for me.

"I don't know what I thought he would be like, or what I thought might happen, but it was so strangely normal that I remember feeling disappointed. Here was this stooped, ailing man in his sixties, shaking my hand, inviting me to sit on his little porch with its sagging roof and faded green paint while he waited for me to start the conversation. I remember sighing aloud, which of course I always do under stress, and then I asked how he was doing. Not an auspicious opening."

We laughed and Mama paused to sip her tea.

"We sat and chatted awhile, awkwardly—like the strangers we were. Nothing of much importance. I looked for signs of me in his face. There were none. His eyes were a pale gray-blue."

"And yours are brown, like your mother's."

"Right. Well, he finally got around to saying that he would have liked to have raised me like a real father. He had always loved my mother and wished things had been different. I said I was glad to hear that and wished the same. I kept thinking that I wanted to remember everything to take with me—the look of the house, the smell of the hot July day, the light and feel of it all."

"How long did you stay?"

"Oh, not long. Thirty, forty minutes at most. Eventually I asked him for his picture, but he said he didn't have a recent one. 'Nothing you would want,' he said. He told me then about the only photo he had of me. I wondered where he kept it . . . in a small silver frame on his dresser, perhaps, or fading in a bureau drawer. I told him about you, my Betsy, nearly eleven, pride of my life. I wanted him to ask to meet you, but he didn't.

"I stood to leave. I still felt awkward and ill at ease. He reached out and said, 'I'd like to give you a hug, honey.' I was trembling inside and wished later that I had hugged him better in return. I missed my only chance. As I started down the steps he said, 'Wait just a minute. There's something I want to give you. Let's walk out back.'

"I followed him around the side of the house to the backyard where there was a small garden, just a few rows, squash and pole beans, cabbage, I think. 'Just a minute. You wait here,' he said.

"I shielded my eyes from the bright morning sun and watched him walk over to some staked plants in two washtubs sitting by the old metal garage. He threw his right foot out when he walked which gave him an odd gait. I wondered if it was from an old injury. He returned with a broad smile, his hands full. 'Here,' he said. 'I hope you like these Big Boys.' I took the three large, beautiful red tomatoes he offered. Ah, those are *my* hands, I thought, as he passed me the tomatoes. 'Oh, I will. I know I'll enjoy them. Thanks so much,' I said.

"He walked me to the front and I drove away. I saw in the rearview mirror that he gave me a little wave and watched me to the corner where I turned.

"I began to cry, thought about going back. I wished I'd called him Daddy at least once. I knew I would regret that. And that he and you would never know each other. I hated that it wasn't going to end like a fairy tale, with us all united as one happy family. I looked on the seat beside me and considered that this was the only gift I would ever have from my father, my inheritance: three ripe tomatoes.

"Your grandmother was waiting for me when I got home. We sat in the kitchen and I fixed us both a fine tomato sandwich for lunch. I told her about the meeting, all that I could remember. She listened and asked, 'How did he seem—to you, I mean?' I didn't know how to answer, didn't know what she was hoping to hear.

"Eventually, we joked about my inheritance, part of which we had just eaten. 'Save your seeds,' Mother said, 'and you can plant tomatoes next year.'

"And that's just what I did," Mama said.

"That is so touching. I'm glad you finally told me," I said. "How come it took you so long? I guess he must be dead by now. Did you ever see him again?"

"Oh, no. Never again. Yes, he died about seven years later. When we were in Canada on vacation . . . remember? It was all over and done with by the time we got back." She looked out the window again. "Mother saw his obituary in the paper and went to the funeral. It was graveside. 'Very small,' she told me. The house and what little he had went to hospice. They took care of him at the end.

"And I can't say for certain why either of us waited so long to tell, honey. Afraid, I guess. Mother didn't tell me until both her parents were dead. I think that was the real reason. She said it had been to protect me, but I'm not so sure. And how come I waited? That really *was* to protect me, I guess. Not telling has been a way for me to hold on to that little bit of time I had with my daddy on that one fine day. I could still have him all to myself. I never even told your father. If he were still alive, I believe I'd tell him now."

We were quiet for a minute. She stood up to get a better view of Annie, then turned back to face me.

"But," she said, straightening her back, "I'm glad it's done. Now, then. I've passed on my daddy's legacy to you and before we know it, you'll be telling our Annie, who's out there this very minute proving she loves to dig in the dirt. I'm willing to bet she'll make a terrific tomato grower!"

Mirrored Images

While going through my closet today, I came across my grand-mother's lovely wooden box with a Victorian lady's silhou-ette burned into the top. It holds some small keepsakes from my mother. As I lifted the lid with its tiny brass hinges, I caught the delicate scent of my mother's face powder, and I was twelve again, mesmerized by her daily makeup ritual.

Unless she had somewhere to go earlier in the day, which wasn't all that often, Mama waited until four o'clock every afternoon to have her bath and do her makeup. Like fixing dinner, or cleaning house, each of which was performed on a particular schedule and governed by routine, it was a part of her married life. This ritual was timed so she would be finished just before Daddy got home from work.

Until I was allowed to wear lipstick when I turned fourteen, I would sprawl across Mama and Daddy's bed every afternoon watching the makeup process while we listened to the radio. Mama would stand in her slip and stocking feet, mirror in one hand and pull up the blinds until natural light filled the bedroom from the three-sided bay window that looked out across the deep front lawn bordered by a half acre of planted pines.

By today's standards, there was little makeup involved. She ap-plied no foundation that promised to "smooth, lift, and protect" while it moisturized, erased tiny lines, and diminished age spots, as promised by some products I use. Mama's own fine skin was the basis for her beauty. She had lovely, clear, tawny skin with just a hint of the distant Indian or European bloodline that marked her high cheekbones.

Mama began the process with the dark brown cake mascara, housed in a slender, red plastic box with the tiniest little black brush. She would touch the brush to her tongue, then run it along the mascara and apply it to her brows, then her lashes, repeating the process until she was satisfied. She took her time, holding out the mirror and turning her head this way and the other in the afternoon light.

Her rouge was a medium pink that came in a small, round, gold case with a thin, soft applicator pad. One spot of rouge went on each cheekbone and was lightly spread up and outward with gentle pats of the pad. This was critical, Mama cautioned. Catching my eye in her hand mirror, she said, "Too much rouge and you could end up looking harsh and cheap."

Putting on lipstick was my favorite part. I yearned for the day I would be allowed to wear it. I was fascinated by the way Mama spread the color. Propped up on my elbows, I concentrated as she rolled up the gold tube of red gloss, touching it to several places on her lips. Then, with the tip of the little finger of her right hand, she expertly spread the color until her lips were well defined by "Rosy Red." She put her lips together, pressing them to "set the color," then blotted with a tissue. Holding the mirror at arm's length again, she checked the overall effect. When she was satisfied, she would turn to me with a smile. "Okay? Not too much?" I would assure her it was perfect.

I have never owned a compact of my own, but I loved my mother's. The round, gold top was decorated with scrollwork and the inside mirror had a tiny crack in one corner. The puff was worn, and smelled of the soft powder that was the last thing Mama applied before combing her hair and putting on her dress and heels to greet Daddy.

After she died and Daddy asked my sister and me to help him sort out her things, he invited us to take what we wanted. I took things I loved, though with the exception of her wooden rolling pin with the worn red handles, they were things I knew I would never use. I asked for the floral silk scarf Mama wore under her coat collar, a black, beaded evening bag containing ticket stubs to the last concert she and Daddy had attended six years before, and her gold-toned hand mirror.

Inside the wooden Victorian box that was her mother's, I've saved Mama's two silver bangle bracelets, the gold Elgin wristwatch she was so proud of, her last lipstick and rouge case, and the scroll-topped compact that still smells of her powder.

On my vanity, next to the fancy jars that promise the fountain of youth, is Mama's hand mirror with tiny scratches that show some wear along the beveled edge. I hold it up and face the afternoon light pouring in through my bedroom window. I check my makeup. "Okay? Not too much?"

Ironing Things Out

Growing up, I knew that on Wednesday afternoons, I'd find Mama ironing in either the dining room or the kitchen, depending on the season. In winter, she'd set up the wooden board in the dining room near a wall of windows looking out over the backyard, beyond which was a field that ran down to a creek bordered by piney woods. Occasionally, we'd catch a glimpse of a rabbit foraging in the remains of Daddy's decaying garden. On nice days, the room was cozy, taking warmth from the southern exposure. When the weather turned rainy and cold, I felt protected as we listened to the radio and drank hot cocoa.

I did my homework on the dining room table so I could keep Mama company while she ironed. I loved the soothing hiss of the steam iron and the smell of starched shirts placed on hangers and hung from a knob on the door of the china cabinet.

In spring and early summer, the routine was the same, only with the windows open to let in light breezes along with smells of new mown grass and tea olive, fertilizer, and the miniature gardenias planted beneath the windows. We switched our treats from cocoa to iced lemonade, from cinnamon toast and little donuts to Wheat Thins with smoky cheese spread. Our talks were more animated, Mama's rhythm a little faster as she pushed and pulled the iron across our clothes. They were damp and cool, having been rolled in a towel to chill in the refrigerator overnight.

By July, ironing time shifted to early in the day before the heat took over. Mama moved the board to the kitchen where the morning sun was less intense. There was no air conditioning and the single table fan was little help past noon when the sun was high and the humidity higher.

At nine, we listened to Don McNeill and the Breakfast Club. In my mind, I saw the studio audience briefly march around the enormous breakfast table, then sit to generous plates of scrambled eggs and bacon, all the while watching celebrity guests on stage. Such was the magic of radio.

Come October, we were in the dining room once again, closing the windows as the light faded early and chilly shadows fell across the drying grape arbor in the lower field.

When I married, preparing to leave my parents' house to begin life in a home of my own, I asked Mama for the ironing board. I wanted something special from home to take with me. I remembered all the ironing days as pleasant times with Mama, but it was not those memories alone that prompted me to ask for the old board. The board itself was significant to me. It marked the day my parents met.

When Mama was eighteen, having lost both of her parents and being an only child, she was sent south from the Midwest to a tiny country town in middle Florida to live with some of her father's family, kind aunts whom she had never met.

Soon after arriving, her Aunt Hettie took her on a proper visit to meet friends and neighbors. They visited the Taltons and the McGees that afternoon, ending their outing with the Cottons who lived a short piece down a rutted dirt road. From the front porch, the Seaboard Air Line tracks that ran parallel could be seen across a wide open field.

My granddaddy and uncles were all railroad men, flagmen, then station masters. Daddy was the first to go to college. As it happened, on the day of the visit, Daddy was home from the U of F for the weekend.

After the front hall introductions were made, Mama was left on her own to wander about. She walked the short hall to the glassed-in back porch where, standing in his shorts and undershirt, his right hand gripping the iron as he pressed his pants, she met my father for the very first time.

When Grandmama died, Mama asked for the ironing board. And now, I wanted it for my own. Despite how difficult it must have been for her to part with, Mama gave it up.

In the next few weeks, I set up the board once a week on my scheduled ironing day, but something was missing. Ironing alone in a small apartment with only the TV glare for company was not the same at all. So, early one Wednesday morning in April, I took the board home. I traded with Mama for the newer replacement board she had bought.

We sat at the dining room table and shared an early lunch, little Swanson chicken pot pies from the freezer. Then, like every Wednesday, Mama set up for ironing; even the sound of the board being raised was different in her hands. I settled myself and watched as I had done so many times before.

She unrolled the cold damp towel holding a few pieces of ironing and set her bowl of dipping water to the side. Continuing her ritual, she placed one of Daddy's shirts on the board, collar up, lightly sprinkling it with a flick of her fingers.

It was time for the soap operas, so I fixed us each a glass of tea. While Mama ironed, we listened to Our Gal Sunday, the story of an orphan girl from the little mining town of Silver Creek, Colorado, who was married to the rich and handsome Lord Henry Brinthrope. As always, the story asked the question, "Can this girl from the little mining town in the West find happiness as the wife of a wealthy and titled Englishman?" I was certain she could. And here we were, back where we all belonged.

After Mama died, I took the ironing board once again. It seemed fitting somehow, the board having finished its natural progression.

Mother's Day

When I ironed this afternoon, I set up on my back sun porch with a view overlooking the pond where ducks have come to live for the winter. I settled into a comfortable rhythm with my old steam iron hissing time.

"Cocoa or hot tea?" my daughter asked, tossing her schoolbooks onto the nearby table as she turned on the radio.

MAM

As I recall, my mother rarely laughed until she became grand-mother to my brothers' children. Until then, she seemed to take a dim view of things. Perhaps she found her life too hard for humor.

I don't know how Mam coped because she was always in a swivet. She was one of those heavy Irish women with a strong back and rough hands, with graying red hair that flew away from its bun, and a ruddy face that glistened from the ever-present sweat provoked by hard work and the frustration of bringing up difficult sons.

Raising four boys on city streets kept her preoccupied and frantic. The boys were not easy, not one of them. I was the baby and the only girl. I learned early on to be good and keep myself busy and out of harm's way. Otherwise, I wouldn't have made it. My brothers were rowdy and loud. To this day, when it gets too noisy for me, I find myself humming. Now, like then, it is my way to escape.

My brothers, two sets of twins only twelve months apart, were always in some kind of trouble. Nothing that would bring the cops, but pranks and such that kept somebody upset with them at all times. They were unpredictable, either sticking to each other, blood kinship their glue, or fighting amongst themselves.

Mam was weighed down with running a household without sufficient help, and too, she didn't have a natural knack for keeping the boys in line. She adored them and they her, but she was never able to convince her sons that helping with the housework and staying out of mischief were the best ways to show they cared.

They laughed at their own antics and took nothing seriously. Our Poppy, Antonio, was never anything but a friend to them. He didn't have it in him to discipline anybody.

Poppy was a smallish Italian man with curly dark hair and dreamy eyes. He worked as a line cook about four blocks from where we lived. Our cramped apartment was on the top floor in a building of thirty families. Because of the proximity to the restaurant, Poppy was always close by to run and fill a shift when someone in the kitchen didn't show. In a big restaurant, that was nearly every day.

Poppy was always tired and worn out from the heat of the kitchen, but he never complained. When he was home, which wasn't often except for Sundays, he was either sleeping or playing his harmonica on the fire escape. Mam seemed to hate that he did either and very little else. But for us, his children, he could do no wrong.

I loved sitting out with him, listening to the music his breath made as it pushed and pulled through the holes in the mouth harp. I was awed by what his mouth and hands could do with that small reed instrument. Perhaps his music was what had attracted Mam to him when they were young. That and his good looks. Whatever it was that had attracted Poppy to a younger Mam was not obvious to me.

Sometimes on his day off, Poppy would take me with him to the restaurant to pick up his pay. I loved the smell of the spicy sauces simmering in large heavy pots and the sausages roasting in the ovens. Mr. Zambini and his staff were always happy to see me.

My brothers and I craved the fabulous pasta dishes Poppy brought home, while none of us wanted to eat the plain meat and potatoes meals our Irish mother made. I sat and picked at her cooking, but felt badly enough for her that I would eventually eat most of what she put in front of me. My brothers were incorrigible. They made faces and rude noises of gagging and worse. "Please, boys," was the most Mam ever said. Poppy was too soft and removed to get involved. Sometimes he also hummed so as not to hear.

So Mam did it all—the unappreciated cooking and cleaning, washing our clothes and bed linens in the bathtub, hauling the heavy wet wash down five flights to dry on crooked lines that ran across one side of the communal yard. It was an impossible and thankless job, but she did it. There was no need to complain; it wouldn't change a thing.

Except for Poppy, she got us all to mass on Sundays. Weekdays she fought with the teachers and neighbors about her boys. They were known throughout the neighborhood as "those tough Scarlotti kids." Everyone had an opinion about how they should be handled, what made them so unruly, why they couldn't be controlled. In one way or another, the blame always came back to her.

I heard people talk, and sometimes she dragged me along to the meetings at school just to have someone on her side. They said she needed to put her foot down, not allow the boys to run over her, give them a good whack upside the head. Or maybe they needed more of her attention. No one, not one, blamed my father. Antonio was "such a sweet and pleasant man," a cheerful man always working hard to provide. No, it was up to Kathleen, her responsibility, her failing. It was no wonder she didn't laugh.

When my youngest brothers were thirteen and I was twelve, Poppy was splattered by hot grease and his apron caught fire. Both hands and forearms were severely burned. Though his hands gradually healed, they were crippled by thick scar tissue. He could no longer play his harmonica. He never worked again.

Mam said I would have to do more chores. She was proud and would not consider asking outsiders for help. There were lots of relatives but they had nothing to spare, and there were none who lived near enough to even offer consolation.

"It's up to us to figure things out on our own," Mam said. "We'll take in laundry."

It was all she knew to do.

I was sent door to door throughout the building and the neighborhood to find clients. It was embarrassing, humiliating, but I found enough to get us going. And while we were at school all day, there was Mam, washing and lugging other people's laundry, all to be ironed at night when the rest of us had gone to bed. It was up to me to pick up the dirty laundry before school each day and to make deliveries in the afternoon.

Meanwhile, Poppy disappeared into some dark place. He sat silently, staring out our front window into some faraway sky. Mam looked exhausted, her eyes vacant.

When it was evident how things were going to be, I made a brave coming-of-age decision.

One Sunday after mass, while Mam stayed home to keep Poppy company, I told my brothers that Father John wanted to speak to us at the rectory. They moaned and pissed around, but they followed me down the street to the imposing two-story red brick house with three chimneys. I opened the high, forbidding iron gate, marched up to the massive door, and pulled the bell.

Father John greeted us with a quizzical smile. "Well, what a nice surprise. Come in, come in."

"Morning, Father," we chorused.

"So what brings you here? Mary Margaret?" He gestured toward the back of the house. "Come, come. Just follow me."

Michael was the first to realize I had gotten them there under false pretenses. "You lied," he hissed and pinched my soft upper arm. I wheeled around and slapped him and, for a second, I thought he might hit me back. But Father's voiced boomed ahead of us down the dark hallway lined with portraits of the saints and we followed along to the musty den. It was a large dark room, filled with heavy furniture and Roman icons. Shelves lined two walls, filled top to bottom with books and periodicals.

We settled into over-stuffed chairs and a maroon velvet-covered Victorian sofa. Dust motes rose and floated in the light filtered through cloudy windows. I wondered if Mrs. Riley was too blind to see the windows needed washing. Maybe Father didn't own a stepstool. My brothers sat stiffly, eyeing Father's every move. I smoothed my pinafore and stared at my scuffed patent leather shoes.

When Father was seated behind his imposing mahogany desk, I started right in as if I had rehearsed this speech a million times, as if I knew what I was doing, as if I was much older and had full command of my thoughts. While I refused to rub my bruised and stinging arm, the pain added fuel to my fury.

"I need your help, Father. Our Poppy's not well and we have to pay the bills and eat and we need more money. Mam works all hours and I help her when I can, but that's not enough. It's only fair that everybody has to work." I glared in the direction of my four shocked and silent brothers. "These boys won't pay attention to our Mam so you are the one who has to be in charge of them. I'm a girl and just turned thirteen or I would beat them myself 'til they minded me." I stopped, out of breath. My heart was pounding.

Clearly, I might die where I sat.

Father John may have found me amusing, but after a pause he adopted a very serious expression and turned to my brothers. "Well, boys, you've heard your sister. What is it you intend to do?" Tony and Nick, the older twins, recovered first. Hunched over, eyes lowered, they answered, almost in unison, "Don't know, Father. . . . whatever you say."

"I'm glad to hear it," Father replied.

When we left, the boys walked at a fast clip ahead of me, but nobody spoke.

And it was just that easy. Within a week, each of my brothers had some kind of afterschool work and was making a little money to bring home. They changed jobs occasionally, but from that moment on they worked at something.

Mam never knew about our meeting because Father John threatened the four of them with Divine retribution if they told anyone. He also began the habit of coming around unannounced every few weeks "just to check on things." Mam was so grateful for the extra help that she never questioned my brothers' motives, but prayed thankfully that it would continue.

Two years after the fire, when it seemed that life was getting better for us all, Poppy walked to the corner for a paper one rainy afternoon and was struck and killed by a motor bike. The delivery man who hit him had run up onto the sidewalk to avoid a speeding truck skidding sideways on the rain-slick street. Poppy was forty-four years old.

We had missed the happy musical man who disappeared like smoke with the fire that left him helpless, but this was final. We were devastated.

Each of us handled his passing in different ways. I hid out in my schoolwork, determined to make Poppy proud of my efforts, though posthumously. My brothers became less talkative and put in more hours at work. Because they had a little money now, they stayed out later and came home smelling of the nearest bar, all tobacco and alcohol.

Mam was quietly inconsolable.

Within four years of Poppy's death, Nick and Ian, who worked at O'Malley's garage, married neighborhood girls, both Irish and good Catholics. The boys were set to take over when Mr. O'Malley retired. Having put away a little money and coming home to pretty wives brightened their lives. When they moved out, it left Tony and Michael at home with Mam and me. It was good to have a little more space.

By then, I was taking a business course and minding the desk part-time at an insurance company. Soon I would be the full-time receptionist. Among the five of us, we made certain that Mam no longer had to work so hard. Taking in other peoples' laundry was a thing of the past.

Nick and Ian's new wives were good young women with traditional values who insisted my brothers give up their nightlife. The wives stayed at home keeping house and making babies. Within the first year, they had each birthed pretty little girls. Nick's daughter was named Antonia after Poppy and Ian's daughter took Mam's name, Hannah Kathleen.

I ordered hand-embroidered batiste gowns from Ireland as their Christening gifts from me, their Auntie Meghan. We began planning our very first family party.

On Easter Sunday, we all gathered to see Father John and the Bishop preside over a service that brought seven new little members into the congregation. Mam was godmother to her tiny red-haired namesake and I was godmother to baby Antonia.

The families represented at the Christening shared expenses for the celebration after the service. We decorated the parish hall with pots of Easter lilies and narcissus to brighten the colorless room. The Guild ladies lent their finest linens for the buffet tables.

Arrangements we made of white and yellow roses, baby's breath, and ivy were on each dining table. Doorways were draped with white tulle tied with yellow ribbon streamers.

The hall had never looked more festive.

As I came out of the kitchen with a pitcher of sparkling punch, I spotted Mam seated in a rocker holding baby Kathleen. Mam was smiling, and when Father John leaned over to speak to her, I heard the happy laugh that had gone missing for much of my life.

In that moment, I knew. At least in part, it had been that lilting Irish laugh that had attracted young Antonio Scarlotti to the red-haired Kathleen O'Hara.

Eulogy for an ADPi

Mama was an ADPi at Wesleyan where it all began. First, finest, forever. In other words, not just *any* old Alpha Delta Pi, but the best of the best. Some of her friends consider that the most important thing that can be said of her.

I have been a huge disappointment to them since I chose not to join a sorority at all. "What a waste of important influence," one commented. Mama laughed and told me to ignore the remark.

In making suggestions for her obituary, they reminded me that Mama had been married to a doctor (capital D O C T O R) and not just *any* old doctor. Daddy was a KA at Washington & Lee, which means he breathes rarefied air. Not only that, he was schooled at Duke and that well-respected Yankee haven, Harvard. His specialty is radiology, which means he has kept wonderful hours and made tons of money.

Better than all of this, if you can imagine, he is legitimately descended from R.E. Lee himself, grew up in a *real* antebellum home (no nouveau riche look-alike), and his Christian name is followed by a four, one-two-three-four. Robert Edward Page Bannister, IV. Around here, it doesn't get better.

It has been suggested I include that Mama was a lifelong Methodist, a longtime member of the Daughters of the American Revolution, past chairman of the Junior Civic League, and a twenty-five year member of the by-invitation-only Sasanqua Garden Circle.

Could anything more important be said to sum up the life of

this woman? Her friends don't seem to think so, but would not object if I include she was an accomplished pianist, grew antique roses, kept a lovely home, and gave fabulous dinner parties.

Well, that might do for the papers, but not for her eulogy. I don't know. This stuff doesn't fit my idea of an appropriate eulogy for my mother, but what do I know about these things? I'm in my twenties and have absolutely no prior experience along these lines. After all, she is (do I now have to say was?) my only mother and I, such as I am, am (is it now, was?) her only daughter.

Isn't more expected of me, or have I got it all wrong? Is it just that everyone else would be made uncomfortable by anything more personal than these shallow facts? And what about me? Shouldn't I be able to say what I really think or feel about my dear, dear Mama? Would that be *so* embarrassing?

If left to my own devices, I would have to say that Caroline Hampton Bannister was the dearest, kindest, most wonderful mother a girl could have. She was all those things her friends would list, but to me and my brothers, so much more—that they have either discounted or failed to notice.

I doubt that even one of them who enjoyed riding my mother's wave of popularity has considered the tiny, yet significant, kindnesses she passed on to her children, and even to strangers who showed up at our door. Mama had a smile, a touch that we all longed to experience. It was her generosity of spirit that set her apart and made her shine.

I remain fascinated by the breadth of her influence. It was rare when we didn't run into someone who wanted to chat with her, or wave to her, or in some way be recognized by her, if only for the briefest moment. Her popularity was extraordinary.

Once, when we were in England on a search for family ancestors, we encountered people at the Albert and Victoria and again in a small Cotswold inn, who seemed to know Mama and sought to engage her in conversation. My brothers and I teased her, saying she had far fewer than six degrees of separation between herself and the rest of the world. We believed she could go to the wilds of Africa and run across natives or, at the very least, a visiting missionary with whom she would have had at least some obscure connection.

And she was funny and playful. And a bit risqué at times. She told a dirty joke on occasion and liked to surprise her guests with ribald ditties she accompanied on her fabulous grand piano. When we were kids, she encouraged us to make outrageous faces to prove they wouldn't "stick," as we had been warned by our father. She was such fun.

Mama loved the beach and collected bucketsful of shells each summer. Some are displayed in a glass case in the living room. Most are in baskets or on shelves throughout the house. They made her smile, she said, remembering summer days and sandy feet.

When Mama was sick and it became difficult, and then impossible, for her to concentrate on a book, she had me read to her from *Gift from the Sea*. Lindberg's slow, rocking cadence soothed and helped her fall sleep. As the shells on Captiva were being named and described, Mama told me she had once favored the double sunrise, with its perfectly matched halves. Later, she fell in love with the hard-to-find baby's ear and, during the summers, wore one on a thin gold chain around her neck.

She celebrated holidays with the excitement of a child and made a huge to-do over everyone's birthday, including her own. Even this past birthday, with no more dark, curly hair, her eyebrows long gone, she insisted on a bedroom party, complete with silly hats and noisemakers. She drank a few sips of her ice cream shake and blew out the forty-seven candles on her birthday cake with wishes, including one for luck. She had us string the party pictures along the top of her bed so that she could "reach up and touch happy times."

Christmas will be impossible this year.

I know that eulogies are old-fashioned and can be painfully

embarrassing, as grief-stricken family members stand in front of the church or casket, mumbling and sobbing through vague wanderings, leaving the crowd of mourners to wonder how well the speaker actually knew the deceased, and wishing they themselves had skipped the service and gone off to the golf course or to shop at the mall.

There is a hot, sweaty kind of embarrassment to these performances which puts an uncomfortable edge on an already dark occasion. After such a display, there are those who, out of duty I suppose, feel compelled to congratulate the speaker, to let them know they did "such a nice job" and that "so-and-so really would have been proud." Others remain so miserably embarrassed by the performance, they don't even bother to go by the deceased's home to pay their respects, leaving it to those who do to hang around far longer than they ever intended, causing them to become exhausted and pissy or just very drunk by the time they're able to escape.

All this said, and with no consideration for my brothers' wishes, I still maintain that I cannot bury Mama without a few words. In an effort not to embarrass everyone, I will do as she taught me when I was young and afraid of speaking in front of company or my classmates. I will stand in front of the bathroom mirror and practice, practice, practice until I have it down well enough to move into my bedroom. There, dressed in the exact outfit I will wear to her service, I will stand back from the mirrored door to get the full impact of my performance. Caroline Bannister would be proud to know I haven't forgotten how to do this.

Daddy's thoughts don't really enter into our plans. He left us all about four years ago, having suffered an apparent breakdown which drove him into the arms of an older, rather plain woman who works in the pharmacy where he gets his Prozac.

My brothers—both of whom stayed home from college this semester—and I hardly ever see him. He appears to have lost the brain connectors that tie him to us in any significant way. It's a strange phenomenon, but nothing we waste time thinking about. He was never at home much anyway.

To be fair, I have to say that, until she died, he continued to provide for Mama's every financial need, even through the two years of radiation and chemo which were expensive and have ended quite badly for us.

Six weeks ago, Daddy came to visit her for the first time since her diagnosis. He sat with her for over an hour by the bed where they lay together as a couple for twenty-eight years. I was home at the time and heard their muffled talk and small, intimate laughter as I passed in the hallway.

After that, he was there for a part of every day or evening. The boys and I acknowledged him, but little more than that. It was too late and there was nothing to be said that could make any difference. I continue to wonder what his plain-faced lover must think about all the attention he paid Mama. Perhaps she doesn't know.

Up until a week ago, Caroline Bannister continued to fight valiantly to exhibit some of her remaining self, but it had been a long, exhausting battle against a rampaging enemy. She fell into a coma for the last seven days of her life. And who could blame her? She had been an uncomplaining trooper to the very end.

I realized the scope of my anger with my father when he spent so much time at her bedside in the last days while she was hospitalized. Fairly or not, I looked on this as his attempt to make up for all that he had failed to provide for her, for us. That is, everything *beyond* prestige and money.

As it was too late to change any of that, I concluded his histrionics could only serve to salve his suffering conscience. I'm sorry, but I care nothing about that.

My anger escalated and took on deep roots as he fell into fits of crying over Mama during her last comatose days. I considered that she might have escaped into her sleeping limbo in order to avoid such unwelcome drama. He was seeking redemption and she was far too frail to offer him further forgiveness or comfort.

The funeral for my beautiful mother is scheduled for day after tomorrow at 10 a.m. at Holy Oaks Cemetery, which in itself is already a disappointment to the ADPi's. They think it should be held at the church sanctuary, full blown, with organ processional and doves descending. The boys and I have opted for a simpler service. Mama left it to us to plan and I know she'd approve. She had a very definite streak of non-conformity that I might possibly have inherited. It is my brothers who got her good looks and kind heart.

I'll begin to practice my eulogy tonight after the house has emptied of well-meaning friends and relations. By Wednesday morning, I'll know it well enough to perform without the 3-by-5 notecards which some depend on.

I'm not yet certain of all that I will say. I'll try to keep it short and sincere. I'll base it on my brothers' and my experience of her and speak of how we loved her and she us, how desperately we will miss her. I intend to share a few words about how amazing she was and her impact on our lives.

I will do my best not to cry.

And, of course, I'll be kind to her friends as she would wish. After all, their lifelong associations were important to her and they were instrumental in keeping up her spirits and ours during her illness. She would expect me to display the same poise and grace they had in common.

As I stand to say a few words in front of the people she loved, I'll wear her baby's ear shell around my neck and, in my right hand, I'll clutch an Argonauta from her collection. Like Jason, as he began his voyage in search of the Golden Fleece, I'll pray for favorable winds and a safe passage.

And for those special few, I'll be certain to add that, until the very day she died, Caroline Hampton Bannister remained a loyal and devoted ADPi.

Shades of Grey

It was early. The tiny kitchen smelled of squirrel guts, the fresh entrails laid out on the spread newspapers. Daddy had been in from hunting about half an hour and so far had stripped four of the animals of their soft, brush-like fur. Through the single kitchen window, we watched the sun peek into the cold grey morning and, as if finding it wanting, slip away until another day.

It was early February and my sister's fourth birthday. She had requested fried squirrel for breakfast. She was too young to realize they were the same cute furry little creatures she chased up the pecan tree in our backyard.

Mama hated the whole project. She couldn't stand the pungent smell or the taste of the fried meat from bushy-tailed rodents that scurried around the yard, grabbing the pecans, chewing her clothesline, digging in her potted plants, then racing to the treetops to perch and screech like monkeys. Most of all, she hated the mess in her kitchen.

To go with fried squirrel, we had to have biscuits and grits. It was too much too early and there was no space. No space to roll the biscuit dough, no room to work with all the mess of gutting and frying squirrel. Too much going on in her kitchen. She let us know she didn't like it one little bit, but because it was her baby girl's birthday, she would do her best to tolerate the intrusion.

I watched the whole process, from the pocket knife coming out of Daddy's khaki hunting jacket through the skinning and gutting, with my chin resting on the counter.

"Move back or you're going to get splattered. Go on, move it. You're not going to miss anything."

Daddy spoke sharply and I moved back. It was always like this. Terrified I was going to miss something, I got too close. Too close to the counter, too close to the knife, too close to the frying pan of hot grease. Always a tug-of-war with us: my wanting to be in the middle of the action, to see it all; Daddy wanting me out of the way, partly to protect me, partly because I was a nuisance.

He washed the squirrel carcasses under cold running water, his large hands cleaning them inside and out, their naked pink bodies looking like small, skinny cat corpses. I saw this, but didn't care. Nothing could take away the pleasure of this fried delicacy. It was better than the wilder game that came through the kitchen in much the same way, to be skinned or plucked. Squirrel might have its own distinctive smell, but it wasn't wild and potent to the taste like turkey or venison or duck, and squirrel was never as tough.

Mama protested all of it, but on different grounds. "What kind of person would eat deer?" she wondered aloud, having recently seen Bambi's mother shot down in cold blood. "And turkeys. Who do they bother?" They were just great big lumbering birds with pretty feathers, and for Thanksgiving, that you could buy at the grocery and didn't taste of its native diet and chew like leather. And the squirrels? "Well, they're just grey and irritating," she said.

When the preparation was over, Daddy rolled up the dirty newspapers and took them to the garbage can out back. Before he was out the door good, Mama had wiped down the short counter and scoured it with Dutch Girl. The bowl of biscuit dough was waiting to be rolled and cut with the rim of a juice glass into rounds that would rise to great heights when popped into the 400-degree oven. Within minutes, the smell of the baking biscuits displaced any lingering odor from the raw squirrel. The atmosphere began to change.

Grits popped against their lid while I set the table and Mama heated lard in the large cast iron frying pan. Daddy shook the brown paper bag partially filled with flour and seasonings, dropping the squirrels in the bag one at a time. After the grease was hot, he sprinkled flour across the surface to check the readiness. When the flour sizzled, in went the meat. It was left to Mama to make gravy.

When everything was ready, Daddy woke our birthday girl and the four of us sat down to eat. Hot biscuits with butter and cane syrup, fried squirrel with gravy and buttered grits. I said the blessing and I'm sure we were all thankful, but for different reasons: Daddy, because he had supplied the squirrels like he'd promised; my sister, because she was getting her birthday wish; I, because I got to watch it all and eat; and Mama, because this ritual was over for another year. When I finished my "God is great, God is good . . ." she added, laughing, "And dear God, please, for their sake, don't let either one of these girls marry a hunter!"

But we were girls from a family of a long line of hunters, so in time, of course, we did.

GREAT AMERICAN LADIES

I've spent the last seventeen years of my life working for the Department of Family Services which has, just since I've been there, changed its name three times. Each and every time, it means new stationery, new signage, etc., etc., etc., all of which costs the taxpayers money, money, money. I might not care as much if I worked in another department, one where I never met the underprivileged public. But every day, I see firsthand what most people don't see in a lifetime: families, especially children, in serious distress who need that money the state is spending on new, more appropriate, politically correct names for an agency which is understaffed, overworked, and ill-equipped to handle most of what comes across our desks.

When I consider my own childhood, I know I have lived a charmed life. The worst thing that happened to me was really nothing. Although it doesn't begin to compete with the horrors I encounter every day on my job, it seemed like the end of the world at the time.

It was a Sunday morning in early June 1943. A group of ladies, dressed in their summer voiles with pearls at their necks and white-gloved hands, stood gossiping on the steps of First Trinity after the eleven o'clock service.

My parents had gone home after Sunday school and I was in the side church yard with Tildy Spence. We had been playing tag and were now spinning ourselves silly on the tilt-a-whirl. When

Mrs. Spence called that it was time to go, Tildy grabbed my hand. "C'mon, let's see if you can come home for dinner. I'll let you try my new skates."

I ran behind Tildy, laughing and wheezing from the exercise. I waited as she pulled her mother's sleeve for attention, "Mama, Mama."

But Mrs. Spence was busy listening to the other ladies. She turned with a snap. "Tildy, please. Can't you see we're talking?"

Tildy rolled her eyes at me. "I know it'll be okay," she whispered.

We waited, crouching nearby, drawing tic tac toe in the sand. I heard my mother's name and jerked my head. I'd missed the first part, but then Mrs. Spence replied as clear as day, "Well, I think there's probably nothing wrong with Thelma Davis that some charm lessons and a new set of teeth couldn't fix! Eleanor Roosevelt certainly has nothing on her!" The ladies laughed.

Heat, like a runaway fever, spread over my face and neck. There was no misunderstanding her meaning. Looking down to acknowledge her daughter, Mrs. Spence saw me staring at her, mouth agape. "Oh, my," she said. Tildy turned and looked at me for one brief moment. Then I was gone.

I flew as fast as my legs would take me. I ran south past the post office and Mike's Cafe where folks were gathering for lunch, past Lumpton's Hardware and the five and dime. I didn't slow down until I got to the school. It was against the rules to be on the grounds when school was out, but I didn't care.

I didn't fully understand why the ladies had made fun of my mother, but at that moment I was too mortified to think.

All I knew was that I had just lost my best friend. Never again would I get to go home with Tildy Spence. I would never get to try her brand new skates with the red leather straps.

I sobbed and stomped around kicking up dust, then twisted in the swing until I got dizzy and threw up. Eventually, I thought about the time and what Mama would say. I used the water fountain to rinse my mouth and face. On the long walk home, I prayed that I wouldn't run into Tildy or any of the mean, gossipy church ladies.

Mama met me at the kitchen door, wiping her hands on her checked apron, demanding to know where I'd been. I told her I'd spun around too much and gotten sick and had to rest on my way home. That made perfect sense to Mama who believed I could never do anything within reason. Given the chance, she *knew* I would eat too much and get a stomach ache and run so fast I'd get a stitch in my side, so she wasn't surprised to hear I'd spun myself sick.

"Just as I suspected," she said. "Go wash up for lunch and see if you can't control yourself for the rest of the day."

I lay in bed that night chewing my fingernails, praying for a plan. I couldn't, wouldn't tell Mama what had happened. I knew I was going to have to have a pretty good reason for not seeing Tildy. It wasn't going to be easy. When I said my prayers, I thanked God it was summer vacation so that I didn't have to face Tildy at school the next day. I asked to be forgiven for deceiving Mama.

A couple of days passed before Mama asked about Tildy. I crossed my fingers and said I "thought" she and her family might have gone on vacation.

"No, ma'am, I don't remember where. . . . just on vacation."

"Well, that's nice," Mama said, "but it can't be too far with the gasoline shortage. You'll be getting a card from her any day now and then we'll know where they've gone."

The following week, my Alabama cousins came to visit. We went to the movies every day or to swim at the lake. Soon, the pain of losing Tildy began to ebb. Before I knew it, June was gone and it was the fourth of July.

We had a neighborhood picnic with hotdogs and lemonade and three watermelons. Later in the afternoon, before the band concert at Owen Memorial Park, I helped Daddy crank peach ice cream in a wooden churn, melted ice and coarse salt spilling over the sides. After the ice cream had "settled," as Mama put it, we walked to the park which was only a few blocks from our house. Mama took citronella to rub on our ankles and behind our ears if the mosquitoes came out.

As we stepped up the bleacher seats, Mama said, "Kay, I see the Spences over there. Why don't you go and ask Tildy about their trip? You never did get a postcard, did you?"

"No, ma'am."

"I guess she was too busy," Mama said. "Why don't you go over and find out where they went."

"Yes, ma'am, after I cool off." I felt sick. My lies were about to catch up with me.

When we were seated, Daddy went to buy Coca-Colas and peanuts. I held my breath, waiting for Mama to make me go speak to Tildy and Mrs. Spence.

She leaned forward and looked across me. "That's odd. Mildred Spence just snubbed me. I waved and she looked me straight in the eye and turned away. What in the world?" I didn't say a word.

"Katherine," she said, drawing my name out slowly, "is there something I should know that you're not telling me?" She took my face in her hands and looked me in the eye. "Is there? If so, you'd better tell me right now."

"No, ma'am, there's nothing you should know," I said. "I promise I'd tell you if there was."

She squinted at me for what seemed an eternity. I swallowed hard, trying not to break my stare. Apparently satisfied, she loosened her grip.

"Well, I know what I saw. And Katherine, I don't think you should plan to play with Matilda again. I don't want you to continue a friendship with someone whose parent has such rude manners. I know it will be disappointing, but I don't care to discuss it. Here comes your father. Let's see if we can't enjoy this music."

Daddy handed out the Coca-Colas and peanuts, boiled ones

for him and me, but because Mama considered these too messy, parched for her.

The salty peanuts stung my mouth. I hadn't realized I'd been biting my lip. I breathed a sigh of relief and said a silent "Thank you, God."

Until this day, I hate the thought that Mrs. Spence slighted my mother, but if it was so, I know it was out of guilt over that snide Sunday morning comment. Mama only mentioned Mrs. Spence's slight one other time that I recall, and that was on our walk home that evening. Daddy listened to the retelling, then reached over and put his arm around Mama's shoulder as they strolled along ahead of me.

"Oh, Thelma, why would anybody want to snub my girl? Don't you worry your head about Mildred Spence or anybody else. I hope you won't let it bother you even one little bit."

As was true throughout their life together, Daddy's calming words were all that was needed to soothe this or any other upset for Mama.

By September, Mr. Spence, who must have had better eyes than my father, was drafted into the Army. Tildy and her mother followed him to Kansas to be close to his base. We never saw or heard about them again. By Christmas vacation, I had found another best friend.

Beth had come to live with her grandparents for the rest of the school year. As it turned out, she stayed for three. We were a perfect pair. I knew it when she walked into class with her new braces and eyeglasses just like mine. That she liked to skate and read a book a week was almost too good to be true.

As for Mrs. Roosevelt, she became respected the world over for her good deeds, her great courage and intelligent insights. She pushed against her natural shyness that caused many to think of her as uppity and inept in the early days and became a working ambassador for the underprivileged, beginning with the poor just beyond the White House windows. Following her lead, my equally shy mother volunteered with our local mission where she organized help for the needy for as many years as she was physically able. One could argue that I took up the banner.

Except for a few long-forgotten newspaper caricatures, little was made of Mrs. Roosevelt's toothy smile and pronounced over-bite which, with better dental care, actually changed over the years. Regardless, I think she photographed best when laughing her great inclusive laugh.

Through the years, I have been told by more than a few people that they were reminded of Mrs. Roosevelt by my generous and charming mother. I smile and thank them and feel genuinely proud and fortunate to have experienced the influence of both of these great American ladies.

Meanwhile, I still hear about things that would make your hair stand on end, and I visit documented hardship cases that make me squirm and toss in my bed at night. I think about how lucky I and most of us are, and wonder how people in such dire circumstances can possibly survive to become "worthwhile, productive citizens" as they say in my business.

Relying on the example set by these two good women, I do what little I can by continuing to dole out food stamps and advice to poor, unfortunate people while pointing them toward additional places for help, always in the hope they can make it through to a better life on another day.

Trust Factors

Momma has often said that Rulie Adkins is her oldest and most trusted friend. Unlike Rulie, who can trace her family to the first Adkins to settle in South Carolina, and beyond that to her roots in Africa, Momma can't trace her family beyond the front porch steps.

Momma's parents, the adoptive ones who raised her from a baby, were killed just days apart when she was twelve.

Granddaddy died after lying comatose for three days following a head-on collision with a truck full of young drunks who whammed into him following an afternoon of partying at Pedlar's Pond. He'd been out cruising timber on some family property off the old Millhopper Road and was on his way home to my grandmother's thirty-first birthday party.

Four days after his funeral, my grandmother died instantly and alone in a single car collision with a utility pole on State Road fifty-eight. The evidence suggested she had probably hit speeds of ninety-five or more.

"Grief can be blinding," Momma says.

Until then, no one had elected to tell her she was not their natural child. Momma learned that truth while sitting on the edge of her seat, a handsome green leather club chair, in the impressive book-lined office of her parents' friend and attorney, J. Malcolm McDonald. Great Aunt Sophie, her mother's twenty-one-year-old unmarried sister with whom she was now going to share her home, sat to her right in a matching chair.

After the reading of the will and clarification of its contents, J. McDonald said there was something in particular he needed to say to Cass. At this, Sophie got up and walked to the window overlooking the front street where she stood with her back to the room and her niece while the attorney took Momma's family away. According to Momma, Sophie then whirled around and said, "C'mon Cass, let's go." And that was it.

The lawyer McDonald advertised for a live-in helper for Momma and Sophie, someone to cook a little, clean a little, and stay to help "the girls." The idea was that she would be there until Momma turned twenty-one and could take over her own life, the house, and the remaining bulk of her trust.

This October, it will be thirty-one years, and Rulie shows no signs of leaving.

"I didn't cry," Momma said, "but I know I made up my mind then and there that people, especially family, were not to be trusted. That was a terrible thing to decide at such an early age, but it was my response to that tragic revelation."

Sitting on the front steps having drinks together as we watched the sun going down on an early fall afternoon, I thought that "tragic" might be an overstatement. Shocking was probably more like it. But Momma was in her head, remembering that terrible time. This second drink Rulie fixed for us had loosened Momma's memories as well as her tongue.

"Losing Mama and Daddy was impossible to understand. I was in shock for a long time. But the secret J. McDonald told me that day was also devastating. I'd been deliberately lied to . . . by omission, granted, but lied to nevertheless. And then there was the business of having to live for the next umpteen years with the likes of Sophie. I knew that wasn't going to be a picnic."

In her current metamorphosis, Great Aunt Sophie's hair is auburn. It was originally dirty blond. Two years ago, it was the color of the Lady Ligeia's: black as the raven's wing. That was the year she decided to get her first tattoo. How cool is that, I ask . . . a black butterfly on your butt at fifty-three! Sophie lives in Colorado now and has never married. There's been talk that she's as fond of women as men. Rulie says not to trust gossip.

"What was wrong with Aunt Sophie?" I asked. "She's always seemed pretty cool. I'd have thought she'd have been easy to live with, seeing as she was only ten years older than you and kind of interesting."

"Well, sure," Momma said. "It might seem that way now. But at the time, Sophie's age and 'coolness' meant she was mostly unpredictable. And undependable. We never knew when she was coming home . . . or if . . . or what she'd be like when she got here. I suppose I should give her credit for my never wanting to follow in her footsteps and do drugs or sleep around. Oh, Sophie was interesting, all right!"

We sipped our drinks as the orange light spread across the horizon and the air cooled to a chill. I could hear Rulie stirring around in the kitchen. I pulled my sweater tight as Momma continued to reminisce.

"And, of course, my parents loved me, maybe even more than if I'd been their birth child. But none of this registered then. It took years for me to get to a place where I thought I might understand. That didn't come 'til after the grief of losing them subsided—and I came to some acceptance of Sophie. After all, it couldn't have been easy for her. I'd been too turned in on myself to understand. Or care. That's been bitter for me to swallow, how selfish I was in my grief."

"Ten minutes," Rulie called from the kitchen. Supper was almost ready and Daddy was pulling in the drive from a late game of tennis. We stood up to go inside.

"If it hadn't been for my wonderful Rulie, I don't know if I'd have made it," Momma said. "She's what made me want to come out of hiding and live. Her caring and smarts are what put me back together." Momma reached for my hand. "C'mon. Let's go eat. Don't want supper to get cold."

⁓

Momma claims that she and Rulie took to each other at first sight. For Sophie, it was another matter. Sophie was as unlike her deceased sister as you could imagine, Momma says, and didn't care who came to stay, as long as they did their job and didn't cramp her style. Grandmother had been tall and slender, with dark hair and a radiant smile. Her nickname was Sunny, her attitude reflecting her name or vice versa, Momma says. She was the responsible sister.

Rulie says that when she showed up for her first day at work, she met a nervous young Sophie who wasn't particularly friendly, but had reasons, Rulie reckoned. Seems her sister had just been killed, which wasn't all that long after their parents had both died of some wicked strain of pneumonia. Now she was saddled with her twelve-year-old niece. It was in the will that Sophie was the one to guardian young Cass in case something unforeseen happened. Well, it had and it was terrible. There was no one left now but Sophie and young Cass. Sophie had encountered so much death it was no wonder she was shaky, Rulie says. "Knowin' her history, I could forgive her a lot."

Cass was withdrawn and still in shock, Rulie said, so she took pity on the two and decided to stay. She had helped raise six younger brothers and sisters so she wasn't afraid of hard work or a challenge. The lawyer, Mr. J., seemed desperate to get some help for the girls and he was willing to pay more than Rulie could get anywhere else in town. "I tol' him I'd try it on for size and give him my word we'd be there for six months."

Rulie turns fifty next year and still goes like a house afire. She can do the cleaning, laundry, and three meals a day with her hands tied. All the while, she does this little whistling/humming thing that makes you think she's having a good time. I asked her about this when I was a girl and she said, "Might just as well enjoy whacha do 'cause there's no gettin' 'round it." Good advice, but it helps to have the right makeup . . . which I don't. I'm much too easily discouraged and prone to dark moods. Rulie is also very organized; I'm not that either.

Besides taking care of Momma and Aunt Sophie, Rulie stayed on when my folks married to take care of them and then me. Daddy says when Rulie goes, he goes. He's more than fond of her. He says she's the smartest one in the house. High praise from a man who was class Valedictorian in high school and graduated from Auburn with honors.

Daddy's a small animal vet in partnership with his older brother, Jack, who specializes in large animals. Everybody loves them. Between the two, they've got animal care sewed up around here. I'm their right-hand help, so I know. I've been there a few years now. I'm being forced to work on that organizational thing, as well as my dislikable personality traits. I've even caught myself humming sometimes. I should tell Rulie.

Rulie says it was the animal connection that brought Momma back to life. Momma got Sallie as a puppy soon after her mother died. It was Rulie's idea. "Animals and books," Rulie says. "I knew those'd help her to heal."

Sallie was a mixed collie and grew up to look like a movie dog. When she was six, she got her paw caught in a street grate and ripped the skin. Momma and Rulie took her straight to the new vet. Daddy was just out of school and happy for anything that came through the door. He says it was love at first sight for him . . . for Momma and for Sallie. It took longer for Momma to decide how she felt because of her major trust issues. It was the way Sallie took to him that eventually convinced her that Joe Hamilton, DVM, was worth her time.

Momma was eighteen and Daddy twenty-four when they met. He was only the second guy she had dated. No matter; the first time he came to the house to pick her up, Rulie says she knew when she saw them together, it was the real thing. "I could tell he had healin' hands."

Daddy says he thought he was going to be an old man by the time Momma agreed to marry him. "Cass kept me waiting till I was dang near thirty!" he laughs. That's an exaggeration, of course, since they married three and a half years later when she was twenty-one and he, twenty-seven. She wanted to wait until she felt she knew for sure, until she had passed her big birthday and come of age . . . until she was in charge of her trust money and her life. I was born three years later.

I think Rulie was right about Momma and Daddy being suited for each other. He was looking for someone to take care of and she needed someone kind, a trustworthy man. But it didn't necessarily follow that because they meshed, she would be a good mother. It wasn't that she didn't love me. She was just inattentive. Preoccupied with her own pursuits, she left me for Rulie to raise. That was all she knew to do. Lucky me.

Over the years, Momma has played around a little with writing, gotten two essays published, in fact. But she's really a reader. It was those books that Rulie insisted would help bring out the young girl in hiding that influenced Momma in that direction. Every Saturday morning, they would walk downtown to the library. While Rulie waited out front, blacks not being allowed inside, Momma would check out another week's worth of reading. As she finished a book, Rulie would take it along to read at night when she was alone in her room.

We are each aware that Rulie's devotion is what has made our family work. By day, she gave her all to "her girls" and later, to my parents and me. But at night, when the time became her own, she set that life aside and turned to the world of books. Thus began the real and long education of Rulie Adkins that continues to this day. Daddy's right to trust her smarts. She's learned a lot from all those books she's read in the last thirty-one years.

HEART OF THE FAMILY

Jessica is forty-seven, Prissy forty-three. I'm the youngest at thirty-six. It doesn't seem like a big difference in ages, but it's enough to give us differing opinions about our parents. Mama, in particular. Daddy died eleven years ago during his third marriage. Much about what we remember of him has changed. We've either forgotten or forgiven. Mama recently joked that the same would be true when she's gone. She just wants to live long enough to see it!

I'm the baby and admit to being spoiled. For one thing, there was more money available when I came along. Also, Mama was tired from arguing with my sisters and just gave in to what I wanted. And Daddy? Well, he gave in because he felt guilty . . . probably because he was. It was great for me. I got pretty much what I wanted, did pretty much what I wanted and didn't have to fight about it.

I also spent more time with our parents once my sisters were up and gone. I know I had it best . . . until the divorce. By then, I was a senior in college. Even so, it felt like my family had shattered and my home had been destroyed while I was away on a four-year vacation at Georgia. After Mama, I was the one who took it the hardest. When I found out about 'Bobbi,' the new girl—excuse me, *woman*—in Daddy's life, I felt betrayed. I hate to say woman because she was barely older than me, just twenty six. Ugh!

My sister, Jessica, had three boys about to become teenagers, so she was caught up with them and her life as the wife of a boring insurance executive. They'd been transferred to Portland, Oregon, way across the country, so she was removed from it all. She heard about everything by phone or through the mail, while Prissy and I were here in Atlanta, on the spot with the drama.

Being the eldest, Jessica considers herself closest to Mama. (Think what she will, I'm Mama's baby and that says it all.) Jessica's messages to Mama were meant to give sage advice that would help turn the tide of events. How she thought any advice she could give would make a difference was beyond me. First, she suggested daily prayer for guidance. Then she recommended Mama get a manicure and pedicure and a black "negligee." She also suggested reading material that would "spice up her personal bedroom experience." Adding some mystery to her life would be helpful and it might be good to "get away by herself" for a couple of days without saying where she'd be. That would really pique Daddy's interest, guaranteed. The only thing that advice guaranteed was that Daddy could spend those days with bimbo Bobbi, not having to deal with Evelyn, his soon-to-be estranged wife!

Jessica's advice reminded me of that Christian sex book that came out sometime in the seventies, all about wrapping yourself in cellophane and using a lot of canned whipped cream. Probably not the best advice for Mama, though well meant.

Little did we know that nothing anyone said or did could affect the outcome. Daddy had decided he wanted Bobbi, his current secretary, and that was that. Manicures, pedicures, and negligees would be wasted on him. Unless, of course, they were on Bobbi. He'd already colored himself gone.

Dear Prissy saw Mama almost every day and was good about including her. She took her to lunch, had her to dinner at home with Bill and their two girls, and did her best to make certain Mama spent as little time alone as possible. Prissy's idea was to keep Mama busy in the hope she wouldn't notice Daddy's increasing absence before he finally left, which he did one day while she and Mama were having lunch at Ruby Tuesday's.

When Prissy delivered Mama home, they found his note on the refrigerator, held by a LOVE IS THE HEART OF THE FAMILY magnet I had given Mama one Christmas. It was typical of Daddy not to notice the irony. And the note? *"I hope this doesn't hurt too much, but I must do what I think is best for all concerned. I'm taking some things with me now. Will send someone to pick up the rest on Saturday. Don't forget to give them my golf clubs in the hall closet."*

Dear Daddy John, ever the thoughtful sentimentalist.

Meanwhile, it was a wonder I didn't cause Mama to have a complete and total breakdown. I called her every morning at seven before I went off to class and then again at night just before bed. I held it together during the day, but in the evenings I fell apart on the phone and cried to her, as if she didn't have enough grief of her own. I was about as selfish as a spoiled child can be. She listened to my ravings and tears and did her best to console me. In return, I asked what she should have done differently, why she hadn't noticed that Daddy was unhappy? How could she have not known? She should have seen it coming. And no, it's not too late. Do something about it . . . now! I cringe when I think what I put her through.

If Mama felt any guilt about the breakup, she surely must have felt vindicated when Daddy's quick marriage to Bobbi failed after less than two years. Bobbi quit her job *and* Daddy, moving on to another law firm and another, younger lawyer. It was unseemly, I know, but my sisters and I shared a conference call during which we drank ourselves giddy with delight. Poor Daddy, nothing!

When he called us together while Jessica was home for a visit a year later, we were not particularly surprised to hear he was gearing up for another round. Sarah, the newest wife-to-be was thirty, an attorney in his firm, attractive, and divorced with two small children. We decided to like Sarah since she had insisted on drafting a pre-nup that protected Mama and us. She seemed genuinely nice and I think that she and Daddy were happy. His heart wasn't up to it, however, and he died of a massive coronary three years later.

For my sisters and me, our mad was long gone by then and we were just terribly sad and regretful that we hadn't been more forgiving, spent more time with him early on. I had real reason to feel guilt and remorse since I'd been his baby girl, the "light of his life." He used to say that. "Here she comes. Little light of my life." I'd give up years to hear that again.

Prissy and I had seen almost nothing of Daddy when he was married to Bobbi, but when the little blond bombshell was gone, we gradually began to take him back into our lives. He and I had brunch on Sundays after early church. Prissy's husband, Bill, continued to play golf with Daddy throughout the whole saga and later, and had finished a morning round with him on the afternoon he died. It was hard for us all. Sarah was particularly generous and insisted Mama sit with the family at the graveside service.

It is puzzling that none of us girls worried much about Mama during the time right after Daddy left her for good. When all was said and done, gone and good riddance had been our take on his finally leaving. Mama would be fine. She'd pick up her life and go on and prove how strong she really was. That's what women do. What other choice did she have? Mama was Mama, and nothing was going to change that or her. We were wrong on both counts.

A few months after Daddy died, Mama said, "With John gone, I finally feel a closure to our life together that has eluded me." She also acknowledged a new feeling of personal freedom. Together, they precipitated change, because change she did.

It was small things at first. She changed her hair, began going to the gym. Then it was church. She claimed she had never liked the Presbyterian Church and absolutely did not believe in the Calvinistic view of predestination, never had. What would be the point of life if it was all mapped out for you in advance? "That could account for a lot of the angry people in the world," she laughed, "the ones who aren't sure they're numbered among the elect!"

She visited other congregations and ended up joining a nondenominational group, which didn't bother me but set my sisters on their ears. It's still a Christian group, I reasoned. "That's immaterial," said Jessica, the strict churchgoer with all the kinky sex advice. "We've always been Presbyterians."

Mama began to travel, first with old friends to places where she felt safe. There was England and then the western part of the U. S. Jessica was outraged that she didn't make it up as far as Oregon to see her. "Not enough time," Mama said, ignoring Jessica's huff.

Once she got her sea legs, Mama took off on her own. Greece, Italy, India, and the former Yugoslavia. "I want to see it all," she said.

On the long flight back from Bosnia, she sat next to a man from D.C. who asked if he might call her when they got home. She agreed, and two days after they arrived in the states, he made good his promise to be in touch. Frank was Mama's age and just getting over a bitter divorce. He worked with a non-profit group that helped find financial aid for foreign orphanages. According to him, his wife could never have babies and she resented the fact that he worked with children all over the world while she sat at home, lonely and barren as the desert.

There's got to be more to it, I thought, like why hadn't they adopted? I was right. Early in their marriage when they were told they could never have children, they agreed to wait a while on the decision to adopt. Time passed and so did the desire to start a family.

Frank was a high-powered lawyer who got fed up with the system one day and chucked it all without consulting his childless wife. He quit his firm and decided to look for something more humane than the legal profession and ended up in his present position. His wife, Claudia, had grown to love the good life that he provided as a successful Washington lawyer, and just because he was fed up with the rat race didn't mean that she was. He could go and do good wherever he wanted, but she was staying put in Georgetown and expected him to continue to foot the bills.

When I heard the story, it made sense to me so I sided with the wife. Mama sided with Frank, of course. This in itself was odd; we'd taken up unobvious and unlikely positions. Fifteen years earlier and our stands would have been reversed. But that would have been before Mama had met and fallen in love with Frank, and before she had decided that personal freedom and exploration were at the core of happiness. And it was before I, now married for seven years, had begun to feel the tattered bonds between my husband and me stretching, before I was afraid for our future together.

You see, I'm organized and crave order, but I also like spontaneity and good food and funky music and movies. Michael's office at home drives me crazy. He never cleans it up. He's a really good guy and I love him to pieces, but he never wants to go anywhere or do anything. His idea of fun is hot wings and beer at home in front of the TV. I'm amazed we ever got together.

Sitting here now, I wonder how Mama and I could have had that disagreeable argument, but there it was: raised voices about what a wife should be able to expect from her husband and whether or not it was okay to switch gears, change course, and renege on promises if he experienced something amounting to a "professional" epiphany. "Commitment beats personal fulfillment," I screeched. I got so angry I stalked away from the house, leaving Mama with her arms folded, her back to me. It was days before we talked again. I waited for her to call and apologize, but it didn't happen. She really had changed. I was left to make the first move.

Jessica, who had yet to meet Frank, decided it would never work for Mama to remarry. "I watched her with Daddy and she was waaay too pliable. She'll end up like that again, doing whatever this guy wants. You'll see. It's doomed from the get-go. You know that as well as I do."

Sounds like your marriage in reverse, I thought. "That's a little harsh," I said. "You're not here to see, but Mama's really changed."

"Well, maybe, but I don't want her to get hurt and personally, I don't want to have to go through another failure with her. My life is finally at a place where I can enjoy doing some things for myself. I don't have time for it!"

I hung up from our conversation wondering if Jessica's church-going did her any good. She sure as heck didn't have much compassion for our mother. It pissed me off. Jessica hadn't even been around during the divorce except by phone. She's Daddy's child, I thought, self-centered and worried about how everything will affect her. Maybe I'm spoiled, but she's egocentric to a fault.

Prissy and I met Frank the second time he came down to see Mama in early October. He was quite good-looking we agreed and seemed smitten. It was strange to think of Mama with someone other than Daddy, but with him dead, it was easier to consider than if he were still alive, albeit married to his third wife.

We had dinner together at Prissy and Bill's new condo near Decatur. They had given up their Northside house when the girls were ready for college. It was down-sizing but also a way to pick up some significant cash to help with tuitions. They were smart like that. Bill, the Emory college professor, and Frank hit it off right away when they discovered they'd been members of the same fraternity and were "brothers." That they were both Scotch lovers sealed the deal. "It takes so little for men to bond," I laughingly told Prissy.

My husband, Michael, is not a joiner and being a computer analyst put him further outside the loop. The others had little interest or experience in computers beyond the basics. He was a good sport, though, and chatted up my mother and Frank, whom he came away liking. "I've got a lot of respect for somebody his age who takes off to do something humanitarian. Seems like a good guy. He and Evelyn are lucky to have found each other." His interest in anything to do with my family pleases me no end.

Prissy went out of her way to make Frank feel welcome, with flowers and great music in the background for a spectacular meal. She was our family's most adventurous cook. No one could beat Mama for good home cooking, but Prissy was the "party girl."

She did herself proud that night with beautiful hors d'oeuvres featuring delicate little crab cakes and beggar's purses filled with a curried lamb concoction and tied with long strands of chives. Having heard Mama mention that Frank liked beef, Prissy grilled a tenderloin, rare and stuffed with mushroom duxelles, Duchess potatoes and steamed asparagus with a blood orange beurre blanc. Her homemade yeast rolls with herb butter were enough to make me happy. The meringues with macerated fruit were almost too pretty to eat, but eat them we did, collapsing into our chairs with great sighs before the after-dinner coffees were served on the recently "pot-scaped" patio. That's what Bill called their landscaping in pots. How could Frank not love us all after such a meal, and how happy for Mama to have at least part of her family show such hospitality.

I called Prissy the next morning to congratulate her on such a wonderful evening. We talked about the honored couple and agreed they looked good together. When I asked what she thought of Frank, really, in terms of a possible husband for Mama, she hesitated, which is not what I expected. Prissy is so easygoing and agreeable, with none of the typical angst of a middle child.

"It's his job, Lou. It concerns me. He's so caught up in his work. Not a bad thing, but it seems to be the center of his universe. And the travel, lots of travel that would separate them."

"Well, I don't see the travel as a problem," I said. "Mama says she wants to see the world."

"Yeah, but it's not the same. I don't know if she'd even be allowed to go with him and I wouldn't think checking out depressing orphanages in foreign places would have much appeal. Besides, I want Mama to be the center of someone's universe. It's time she was cherished . . . before it's too late. She's got this one last chance to love and be loved by the right man."

"You're right," I conceded. "So where does that leave us, or rather, Mama?"

"Couldn't say, sweetie. Guess we'll have to wait and see. 'S'pose we've got to trust Mama to do what's right for her. And regardless, we need to be accepting of her decision. Make sense?"

"Sure. But I don't remember *your* being very accepting of her decision to change churches. That was pretty major."

"That's not fair, Lou. I came around. It was such a shock and right after Daddy died. I thought it was some kind of backlash she'd be sorry for. I was wrong. She seems really happy with her choice."

"I always thought it was sort of brave of her."

"And I don't really care where she goes," Prissy added. "At least she made a decision. Bill and I are still wishy-washing around. We haven't left East Side but that means nothing except we like the minister we've got now. This is terrible, but Bill says 'He gives good sermon'."

I laughed out loud.

"Yeah, well, I don't know where I belong, either. Right now, though, I'm off to Mama's. Call you later."

I drove over to say my goodbyes to Frank. Mama was happy to see me and ushered me into the kitchen where they were having lunch before his flight. I declined an offer to join them.

"You busy this afternoon, Lou?" he asked.

"Not 'til suppertime. What's up?"

"Well, I thought maybe you could take me to the airport and let Evelyn have a nap. Last night was terrific, but we're both tired today. You and I can finish our talk we started, about the series pitchers."

I looked from Frank to Mama who nodded. "Well, sure. Great."

It was agreed I'd pick him up at two. I ran an errand and gave them an hour to be alone before I went back. Frank was sitting in an easy chair looking over the paper when I walked in. Seeing someone other than Daddy in that chair was jolting, but it also seemed okay somehow.

"I insisted Evelyn lie down," he said. "No reason for her to wait around for me to leave."

The ride took about forty-five minutes. We got lucky and didn't hit any hot spots in traffic.

While I drove, Frank talked about himself, his job, and his marriage. When we passed the stadium, he remembered our conversation about the World Series. We talked briefly about the Braves' pitching staff. I asked when he might be back again.

"Nothing's in stone, Lou, but I'm thinking, preliminarily, about making a move here. I want to check into the feasibility before I say anything to your mother. Be my co-conspirator if you will and let me be the first to mention it to her."

So that was why he wanted me for his hire. I was surprised, but then again, not. Mama hadn't revealed enough for me to know just how deep and serious her feelings were or what her intentions might be. Finding out was now at the top of my "to do" list.

On my way home, I called Prissy again. "Well, I can tell you this, Frank's serious. I mean serious." I told her about the ride but not his "conspiracy" comment. "Now here's something worrisome I noticed, Pris. He talked about himself and his work, a little baseball, but except for saying how much he enjoyed last night and meeting everyone, nothing passed his lips that had to do with any of us. He didn't ask the first question about me or any of ya'll. He didn't even talk about Mama. I thought it was a hair self-centered not to show even a hint of interest in us!"

"Maybe," Pris said. "Or maybe we're expecting too much. Or maybe he just wanted to share something with you about himself."

"I hate it when you're right," I said. "That makes twice today." We laughed. "After all, I have to remember that I was the spoiled one doing the listening." We laughed again.

Mama asked Prissy and me to lunch about two weeks later. We met at the Atlanta Country Club which meant it had to be something important. She made her announcement over drinks before we ordered.

"This probably won't be a surprise to either of you girls, but Frank and I are in love. I don't know for certain where that's going to take us, but we're planning to do our future together."

"Wow!" I said.

"Good news," Prissy offered.

"Maybe we'll be here, maybe Washington," Mama continued. "I don't know that I care. I just want to be with him as I much as I can. I thought you should know."

We gave Mama hugs and kisses and offered congratulations. During lunch, we asked a few innocent questions and let her enjoy her time in the spotlight.

Over coffee and crème brulee with purple plums, Pris said something about love being at the heart of things, that it could help people, especially married couples, through any hard times that might come along. I thought of Michael and me and hoped she was right.

"Well," Mama said, "that was something I used to believe myself, but when your daddy walked out, I realized that wasn't it at all."

"What do you mean?" I asked.

"I thought I had enough love for the both of us, which wasn't true. It takes two. And it requires something else, I've come to believe. One can love and love and love . . . till you can't love any more than you already have."

Plowing ahead, Prissy voiced her concern about Frank's job, his travel schedule. I jumped in and asked about finances; he would obviously be paying his ex-wife until she marries again, which might be never. Had Mama considered these things, we asked.

"Well, of course I have," she replied. "And that goes to the point I was starting to make. You have to understand that it goes further than love. Beyond love, it's acceptance that will carry you through, girls. And a little patience helps. But true acceptance is what must be at the heart of it, I've learned. That's true for all of us. And in all our relationships."

Mama paused to sip her coffee. Pris and I waited.

And there it was.

"You see, girls, I can't let this job that Frank loves and the obligations he made to his former wife become things that separate us. They were a part of him and his life before we met and I must accept them, just as he will me and conditions that are mine. Not because I love him, but because I *cannot* love him unless I do."

On my way home, I thought about what Mama had said.

Michael was in his office working away on some new project. Papers were spread all over the desk, books stacked on the floor, wastebasket overflowing. He was engrossed and didn't realize I had come in behind him.

I tiptoed out and tapped at the door. "Hey, honey, got a minute for somebody who loves you?" He swiveled his chair toward the door and gave me a smile. I smiled back. "How 'bout I fix us some wings?"

MOMMA'S LI'L BABY

September 15th

Dear Abby:

I turned thirty this past spring. I know that some women get hysterical at the turn of the clock when their twenties are swept into the past, but for me it was no problem. My near ancestors have led long productive lives into their late eighties and nineties. I see lots of years ahead in which I can get panicky if things aren't working out. For now, I'm happy with my life. I love my job as an art historian and I adore Todd, my boyfriend, soon to be more. Life is good.

After our three years of dating and now living together, Todd's family is coming to visit. They will also meet my folks who moved to the New York countryside about twelve years ago to escape the heat and be closer to me. Momma and Daddy, being transplanted Southerners and wanting to do the hospitable thing, have invited us all to their farm for lunch two weeks from Sunday.

This brings me to the fly in the ointment: my mother's cooking. "Joanna," you might say, "at least she cooks." Well, yes and no. She cooks, yes, but she cooks everything to death. I mean *cooks-it-to-death*, cooks it.

Where Momma grew up, there was good southern cooking and then there was really bad southern cooking. It was the latter she learned, which explains *why* she cooks the way she does. Only cornbread refuses to suffer from her abuse. It is always golden, crispy on the edges, not too thick, tangy with buttermilk, and salty from the bacon drippings. But I digress.

If this meal doesn't cause me to lose Todd outright, it will certainly give my future in-laws pause. They might feel only pity for me and their son or they could spirit him away with offers of Kentucky Fried Chicken in order to save him from such a "tasteless" alliance. You see my dilemma.

I need your help. What should I do to avoid this pending disaster? Please, do us all a favor and DO NOT PRINT THIS LETTER.

Thank you for an early reply.

Joanna in NYC

〜

October 12th

Dear Abby:

I was disappointed not to hear from you, but I suppose you can't personally answer every Tom, Dick, and Joanna. I'm sure you have more mail to handle than they process at the downtown branch of the federal post office. Even so, I thought you might be interested in knowing how things turned out.

We survived the dreaded lunch at my parents' and, I must say, it went better than I expected. Todd, who is crazy about Momma and Daddy, took the lead and served himself first. Mr. and Mrs. Wrinkle and the rest of us followed him through a maze of overcooked food, which included limp gray cabbage, green bean mush, and gummy rice. Everyone was kind and no one gagged. I was so relieved when it was over that I escaped to the bathroom and uttered a sigh of relief so great that the cows in the nearby field must have heard!

The following week, I received a heavy, though not very large, package from Todd's mother and a kind note which read:

Joanna, dear, thank you for such a lovely meal on Sunday. I have written to your parents, but also wanted you to know what a happy time it was for us to meet your family. I am taking the liberty of sending you a wonderful cast iron skillet like your mother's. Now you can season one for your very own use. After all, it is just that sort of marvelous shortening bread your mother served that can keep a husband happy and a family well fed. I look forward to having many hoecakes at your table.

Fondly,

Diana Wrinkle

I suppose the only thing left to do is ask Momma for her recipe.

Joanna in NYC

BEDBUGS

Mama's one of five girls from a Southern family with genera-
tions struck through with eccentricities, which in other cul-
tures, northern and western to be exact, would qualify as forms of
mental illness. We in the South are just kinder and more accepting
of our idiosyncrasies. Easterners are less critical of us because they,
too, have their stories and, most likely, are our cousins.

One seldom has to look far to find at least one example of
strangeness in most any Southern family. For the few families not
so fortunate, stories have actually been invented to create a rela-
tive worth talking about. In our world, embellishment is accepted
as a high form of art, although with Mama's family, it is totally
unnecessary.

Truth be told, I'm jealous of Mama and my aunts because it
seems I've not been blessed with the family gene that compels them
to run about with wild hair flying, leaving people breathless in
their wake. Even my two sisters are what you might call "quirky."

As Mama says, addressing me, "Julia, you may have the perfect
name for some sort of oddness, but sadly . . . you are dull as dirt.
You are *truly* your father's child."

Well, I think that says it all. Even my stable brother, Morgan,
the one off in law school at Virginia, has a wild streak running
through him. He was always the first in line to throw paint on the
SAE Lion when he was at Georgia and to bring the grain alcohol

for the purple passion. Whether it will progress beyond that into something really interesting, only time will tell.

They say that Mama's granddaddy, the druggist who ended up dead in a single-car collision with the courthouse steps in Madison back in the '30s, is the same man who wooed his future wife from the top of a borrowed—some say stolen—horse-drawn milk wagon that should have been delivering two cream-topped quarts to Abigail Warren's house early one morning in May of 1923. When he arrived at great grandmother Abigail's home, he stood up in the back and hollered for her to get up and come on down to the back entrance . . . John Marshall was ready to get married.

And she did just that. She jumped up and threw on her clothes, without the required underpinnings, ran downstairs, banged out the door and swooped up onto the wagon with him, leaving her father bellowing out of his upstairs bedroom window and her mother weeping at the back door.

From there, the couple took the milk wagon into the next county where they were married before breakfast. The women in my family all think it was a wonderfully romantic beginning.

Daddy says, "That's just the kind of thing one would expect from a Marshall. None of them has the good sense to see that would have been a terrible beginning . . . the parents upset, the groom facing charges of stealing a milk truck, the whole town in an uproar with gossip . . . the disgrace of it all. What about *that* is romantic? Somebody answer me."

But nobody answers Daddy. No one cares that he doesn't see the poetry. He's not a Marshall.

My grandmother, Margaret, was the druggist's only child. She was five when he totaled his automobile on the public square, himself with it. Her mother, Abigail, closed up their house in town, moved them in with her sister and brother-in-law at their place in the country and took over running the drugstore. She hired an affable and experienced young druggist to take Great Granddaddy's place while she worked the front and did the books. There was no other pharmacy in town, so he stayed on until he retired or the store closed. I don't remember which.

Abigail proved to be a shrewd business woman who didn't mind long hours and hard work. She invested in a little Coca Cola stock, the proceeds from which keep us all in undies to this day.

She did something else unforgettable and worthy of a real reputation. She left her child and stole her sister's husband. She and her brother-in-law lover moved into the back of the drugstore, leaving her sister, Patty, in the country to care for little abandoned Margaret. It was scandalous behavior, but because there was no other drugstore in town, people continued to spend money with Abigail and Sam. The two put in a soda fountain, served a tasty lunch on weekdays, and ignored the gossip until everyone tired of talking. Despite, or because of, her unorthodox life, Abigail is a heroine in our family album and much admired. In fact, each successive generation has someone named for her. Abigail is my middle name.

So my grandmother Margaret—the one abandoned by her mother, Abigail, and raised mostly by her aunt Patty in the country— married a second cousin on her dead daddy's side, and proceeded to breed. Each time, she prayed for a boy to satisfy her husband so she could stop having sex and carrying babies. I know this to be true because she told me and my cousin Lucinda. She also told us she forgave her mother and her uncle.

"To forgive them was the Christian thing to do. They were just sex-starved sinners," she said. No doubt she had this notion drilled into her by her jilted auntie, who, if you can follow, was my Mama's mother . . . which to my mind explains a lot.

Whatever the reason Abigail and her sister's husband got together, it must have been the right thing for them. They celebrated forty-seven years without benefit of clergy.

The only one of Mama's sisters who isn't raving is named Mae Helen, as is my baby sister, Mae H. That's what we call her, Mae H. Except for Mama. Mama calls her Baby Mae, even though Mae's past thirty.

Mama's name is Pauline and her three other sisters are Annabelle, Louisa, and Agatha, pronounced aGATHa. It is hard for newcomers when first thrown in with the five of them. They are known within the family by their nicknames: Mamie, Polly, Belle, Lou, and Aggie. It takes folks awhile.

Seen at a distance, they look perfectly normal. They are attractive women, three blonds and two brunettes, all beginning to grey. But talk to them awhile and you will understand what I mean. The curly hair takes on a wild unruly look, the nervous little laughs take hold, the nail biting begins and they're off to the races. Ironically, each thinks she has escaped the craziness of her sisters.

Aunt Belle has never cooked a day in her life and eats only canned vegetables, which she warms up and serves on English bone china set out on her banquet-length mahogany dining table. She only drinks distilled water with lemon, which she pours into a fine French crystal goblet. She has Rice Krispies for breakfast every morning, which she floats with watered-down orange juice, also out of a can. She is a big Bible reader and has never married. Except for her friend, Caroline, a retired high school gym teacher, she never shares her table with anyone.

"Nor her bed," says Mama with a smirk.

Lou is obsessed with bargains and buy-one-get-one-free offers. She has a guest room full of boxed and canned goods she's purchased on sale. It might sound smart or frugal, but she lives alone, never entertains, and the expiration dates on most of her stuff has long passed. Occasionally, a can will warp and seep and put out nasty odors. Only then will she give it up to the garbage can.

She was married for about four years, but her husband got

sick from some rancid peanut butter and had to be hospitalized. Shortly after the doc discharged him, he left her, declaring enough was enough.

Aunt Aggie lives in a fine house built before the Civil War. She is a charming hostess and employs the best cook in town. Anyone who can wangle an invitation to her table is lucky indeed. She has had three live-in lovers, which is fine, but she has made them sleep in the help's quarters in case someone should unexpectedly come to visit. We laugh at her charade and the silly tour she does when there *is* an occasional visitor and on family occasions. She insists on walking everyone through her bedroom suite on the first floor so they can see for themselves that she lives alone. There is nothing in the house that even hints of a male's presence, except the man himself.

Even Mae Helen—Mamie—the most normal one of the group, has her little quirks. She just doesn't act out like the others. Being married to a conservative Republican banker may have something to do with her decorum. She continues to work out her inner demons in her back garden where she grows every kind of pink and red rose God ever created. We call it the rose jungle. But then there are her children. Uncle George must really love her to have allowed her to give them names that in our region would be considered traditionally black names. Or he was oblivious, which is more likely. There's Lucinda, Annie Mae, Rufus, and Willie. This was her way of showing silent support for Dr. Martin Luther King, she told Mama.

Polly, my mama, hits somewhere mid-range on the cuckoo scale. She's not actually crazy, but sometimes I wonder about her smarts. Her logic is impaired, and often as not, after a conversation, I walk away shaking my head. She's the writer in the family and is working on a "semi-autobiographical" biography. See what I mean? It's either an autobiography or it's not.

I am a little concerned, but Daddy says not to worry.

"Polly's been at that for about twelve years now. What do you think the chances are that she'll ever get that thing to print? It's as big and unruly as her hair!" He's right, of course. She's never finished a thing she's started. Thank goodness she has good help inside the house and out. Elizabeth and Charm Boy keep everything beautified and running like a fine hall clock.

The sisters talk by phone every day and have lunch together, all five of them, at 11:45 each Wednesday at the Blue Willow. They put aside any strange eating habits and order the special. Then they argue about who's going to pay for the two desserts they share. At least one of them is on the outs with one of the others during the week, but at lunch, in view of the public, no one would know. But as soon as they are out the door, the argument du jour resumes. It's always something stupid, of course. Lou, who loves the bargains, picks on Belle who only eats canned goods, purchased singly. Why does Belle *refuse* to buy in bulk? Such a waste of money, Lou says. Mama, the writer, likes to pick on Aggie about her current live-in.

"If you don't stop changing partners, I'm going to get it all wrong in my memoir and it will be all your fault! I've told you I can remember just so much. Our brains have limited capacities, Aggie, and . . . and . . . there's just so many corrections a publisher is willing to print."

And, Aggie? Well, she sure knows how to get at Mama, who refuses to wear any color shoes but red. If you count sneakers, flip flops, and cowboy boots, she has thirty-four pairs. Aggie says Mama needs at least one decent pair of black shoes with a medium heel that is *not* shiny patent leather.

That comment followed Uncle Barrow's funeral about a month ago. He wasn't really an uncle, but an old bachelor friend of our parents who outlived all of his contemporaries. He was ninety-six.

Our family went to the church and then to the graveside service. Daddy was a pallbearer. The Marshall girls were there en masse. Mamie and Belle and Lou stood slightly to the left of the family whose single row of chairs under the Holcomb Funeral Home tent was only half-filled. Nearly all of Uncle Barrow's family had already passed. The three sisters stood close, all neatly dressed in their black and navy, each holding a rose from Mamie's garden to deposit on the casket. They looked the height of respectability, their hair tamed under dark straw hats. I was pleased to notice that not one of them fidgeted.

Aunt Aggie stood with Mama and me and Mae H. to the right of the tent, with the rest of our group gathered behind us near the guestbook stand. I saw Aggie look down more than once during the eulogy and finally realized what she was focusing on. We'd hear about it sooner or later, I thought. It was sooner.

Following the service, we retired to Uncle Barrow's house where his two nieces and their husbands had arranged a light supper. A small group of about thirty showed up to pay their respects. After getting a cup of punch or a glass of wine, several of us retired to the patio to watch the brilliant sunset.

After her initial barbed comment about Mama's shoes, Aggie continued in a loud voice—she was on her third glass of Merlot, "It's damned disrespectful to the dead to wear red shoes to a funeral, Polly. Everybody knows that."

Mama, who I'm proud to say can always hold her own, sniffed and glared back. "Well, only somebody drunk or crazy as a bedbug would say such a thing, Aggie. What everybody *knows*, sister, is that dead people can't even tell. They're all colorblind!"

Daddy, who adores Mama with all her eccentricities, squeezed my hand and laughed. "That's my girl! Give her hell, Polly!"

I let go of Daddy's hand and stepped away, hoping no one, especially Aggie, would notice my open-toed sandals.

A Jewel in the Crown
of Humanity

For thirty-six years, I taught third grade at the Timothy Hudson Elementary School in the small town of Langston, Alabama. When I began teaching in 1939, I was young—just twenty-three—and idealistic. The school was thirty-five and a touchstone of stability in the community. By the time I retired forty years later, we had shared some significant battles and I had become weary of the fight. I felt as old as the classic red brick schoolhouse itself, only without the recent facelift. My paint was peeling and my timbers had shifted.

It was a socially diverse group of children I taught for the first years. Small town schools were like that then. The children of middle-class families made up the bulk of the student body, but Langston's richer and poorer families were represented as well. That was long before anyone was shipped off to private school or driven thirty miles each way to attend some Christian school whose primary purpose was to promote racial segregation. There was no need, I'm ashamed to say. We were already segregated.

It was a great time to teach, however. I loved my students and I loved the school. Parents believed we teachers had their children's best interests at heart and we were second only to them in helping to guide their young. Our students knew we held the authority at school just as their folks did at home. With few exceptions, they minded well and were polite as children are meant to be. They were courteous to their elders and knew to say "yes, ma'am" and "no, sir," without question. Sitting alone in the cloakroom facing the wall or being asked to stand on one leg for an hour beside one's desk was usually all it took to correct a wayward attitude. Being sent to the principal's office was still feared as the worst kind of punishment, outside of a switching at home.

There were exceptions, of course. I dreaded having one of the four Rupert boys in my class—and over the years I had them all. They were dirty and learned their manners from their drunken father who, in this day and age, would probably be reported to the authorities. I know he beat them regularly which gave them cause to curse and push around anybody who got in their way. I found the best way to handle them was to give out special assignments and small jobs.

One year, I think it was Bobby I sent to the library to research birdfeeders and how to construct one for a window outside our classroom. I got one of the other boys to help him build it and then put Bobby in charge of keeping it clean and full of seed. I had no trouble with him the rest of the term and was gratified some years later to spot him working at the local garden shop, in charge of all the plants.

Then there were the Callaway twins, prissy little girls who liked to terrorize the other girls who walked the same way home every afternoon. I had to call their mother in for a conference to put a stop to that.

Overall, though, things were less complicated in those days. Every morning, we read from the Bible at early devotion, which followed the Pledge of Allegiance to the flag. We even said a little blessing at our class table before lunch. No one questioned or complained or appeared to be damaged by these rituals.

After recess, when we returned from the playground, mid-morning break was passed out on a brown pressboard tray by one of the lunchroom helpers. While I read a chapter or two from *Mary Poppins* or the whole of *Snip, Snap, Snur in Candy Land*, the children snacked on Ritz crackers and small glasses of lukewarm pineapple or tomato juice.

By third grade, each child could recite the Ten Commandments by heart. They were listed on the side chalkboard as a reminder. I even taught a Bible verse to correspond to each letter of the alphabet. Every term, it was a race to see who would be first to memorize them all. Then we would discuss what they meant. They learned, for instance, that A: "As ye would that men should do to you, do ye likewise unto them," meant that participating in the drive to collect canned goods and clothing for the poor was a good thing, and that teasing the dirtiest child in class was wrong and would not be tolerated. It was a good lesson and most of my children understood the meaning. Certainly, no one was the worse for it.

Children had a sense of pride in school and country in those days. Mine could find pale green Alabama on the worn, pull-down canvas map of the United States, located over the front blackboard. They knew that our state song was written by Mrs. Edna Gockel Gussen of Birmingham and was adopted by our state legislature in 1931. At Friday "auditorium," my third graders could sing "Alabama, Alabama, we will ay be true to Thee," just as well as the upper grades. They stretched their little voices with the rest of us for the Star Spangled Banner.

Except for January, I believe we had a celebration of some sort every month. George Washington surveyed the room from the wall behind my desk as we celebrated his birthday with the story of the cherry tree and a tale of truthfulness. My class could tell you all about the founding fathers and John and Priscilla Alden. The Pilgrims and their Indian friends came alive at Thanksgiving when we had our turkey dinner and paid homage to those who were said to have begun the tradition.

After a reading about Pocahontas and Captain Smith, we gathered in a circle, each of us with a paper feathered headdress we had colored with a handful of crayons and sang "Come Ye Thankful People, Come," raising our song of harvest thanks.

It was hard to see some of these children with their hopeful faces, knowing they would probably not have much to be thankful for during the holidays. And with our more elaborate little performances, I knew there would always be a child whose mother either forgot to send their costume or refused to provide one.

At Christmas, we decked our halls with fragrant pine boughs and native holly. For a whole week, we spent our first hour of the day cutting and pasting angels and stars and construction paper chains that would sweep around the room and lavish our tree with color and glitter. Every parent was given a gift, things constructed from cardboard cartons and small boxes, pinecones and colored pipe cleaners, red and green tissue, sparkle and paste. Again the children sang . . . loudly, with exuberance, for "Up on the Rooftop" and "Jingle Bells," and softly, with reverence, for "Away in a Manger" and "Silent Night." It was magical to watch those expectant little faces and to hear their darling voices.

Each spring, when we celebrated May Day with a maypole dance, we constructed sweet little paper cones with ribbon handles, filling them with wildflowers and maypops to take home to hang on a front door.

The most popular of all the parents' gifts, however, were the end of the year stories I sent home with the children on their last day of class. After I had been teaching for a while, I asked to borrow the principal's Dictaphone. Each child was encouraged to tell a little story that I would then transcribe. The children made colorful construction paper covers for their booklets, binding them with a length of bright yarn woven through the punched holes. The project was such a success that I continued the practice for a number of years.

Some children were shy and had little to say, so I would end up doing a bit of embellishing. In general, the boys were embarrassed by it all and tended to act silly, but even they were thrilled when they held their typed manuscripts. They, as it turned out, usually made the most creative and decorative covers. I know parents who still treasure those gifts of words as their favorite school years' keepsake.

Occasionally, a student would surprise me with his or her story or touch me so profoundly I can still recall the incident. Ruby, of the orange-red hair, was such a child. She had come to us by school bus for the first time that September. I knew nothing about her family since they had never, to my knowledge, been to the school. She was sent to my room during the first week of class. I could only assume from what I observed that this poor child had come straight from a hard life.

Ruby had tried her best during the year, but that had still left her lacking in some basic skills. I had given her extra help when possible, but I couldn't, in good faith, pass her on to the next grade. She wasn't prepared and it wasn't fair to send her along when she wasn't ready. I planned to devote even more time to her during the following term.

I still had not seen her parents, although I had sent notes and announcements home several times. I asked her about the two older boys in overalls and brogans who met her each day before she boarded the bus. "Them's my half-brothers on my daddy's side," she said.

As we began our recording session, I said, "This is going to be a gift for you to take home to your mother, Ruby, so tell me what it is you would like to say to her. Some little story would be nice or you can recall a good time that you have had together. It can be as long or as short as you would like. Let me know when you're ready and I'll turn on the machine."

Shy Ruby with the frizzy orange hair and gnawed-to-the-quick fingernails, arms and legs speckled with impetigo scars, sat silent, blinking her naturally red-rimmed blue eyes. It occurred to me that she might just be the one child who would never utter a word. But slowly, softly, in a trance-like voice, she began to speak.

∽

"Me and my momma, we're jest alike. Miz Essie Coulter says we're like two peas in the pod." A little smile crossed her sun-blotched face. "I like to think on that . . . me an Momma bein' two peas together. Her and me are both jewels. She goes by Pearl and me, I'm Ruby . . . get it? Me and her like to pet the kitty and she's good to play "Button, Button" with me on the front steps. She don't never get too tired of playin' at that like them others do.

"One time, me and her went to the springs and set in the water. It was real cold and Momma's lips turnt blue and mine too. It set us to laughin' with our teeth chatterin'. Momma's good to show me how to do things. She shown me how to treadle her ole' sewin' merchine and we set there all of a mornin' just puttin' scraps together makin' me and her little lacy collars to put at our necks for our Sunday dresses."

Ruby twisted in her chair and scrunched up her shoulders. She took a deep breath and a little frown developed between her eyes.

"Sometimes jest her and me and Baby Sam used to go down the road to the Padgett place to hitch a ride to the store with Aunt Dolly. Momma always got me a red stick sucker and she'd of got Sam one for his own self, but he was nothin' but a baby. He couldn't of helt on to the stick noways and mighta choked hisself besides. I give him licks offin' mine. It was a good time when we went.

"Sometimes it makes me real sad to think about Baby Sam, but Momma says we can jest go out to the chicken yard and look up and think on 'im. He's up in the sky with baby Jesus and Granpa, but not Rufus. Rufus, he's in cat and dog heaven. I think that's some'eres near to the reg'lar heaven. Momma says we don't have to jest go to the chicken pen, but that's as good a place as any.

"Baby Sam, he was followin' behind while I was pickin' up eggs that last mornin'. I stumbled on a nest out under that old bush out back that didn't nobody know about and he went to pickin' up them eggs and throwin' 'em, and when they busted, he laughed so hard I jest let him keep on bustin' them secret eggs.

"Baby Sam took sick that week with a bad fever, and even when the doctor come, they couldn't do nothin' but keep him washed down. That next Tuesday, he died of lung affection. Me and Momma cried so hard we liked to of died ourselves. It made us sick to our stummicks. I think on that near 'bout every Tuesday. I jest cain't help it.

"I took to worryin' about all them eggs I let Baby Sam waste, so I tol' Momma. She said it was the best thing I coulda' done with them eggs and it made her smile. I was proud I tol' her. That's prob'ly why me and her go to talk to Baby Sam in the chicken yard. I hope Momma likes my story and it don't make her cry none."

∽

The following fall, there was no sign of Ruby or her brothers at school, so I was left to wonder about her and what her mother thought of the story.

Over the years, there have been other students who caused me to consider whether I had made any difference. Occasionally, I'll run into one now, working a low-paying dead end job and question what they might have taken away from my class that has mattered. Maybe just learning their times tables was enough.

I'm glad not to have to go hat-in-hand every year to ask for more classroom money from the administration, not to have to argue against some bigot for the protection of certain books they want to burn, whether literally or figuratively. I can hardly believe the state as a whole survived integration and I might never have chosen to teach had I known that divisive fight was coming.

That and fighting for pay raises took a toll that caused me more than once to consider leaving.

But I couldn't quit. Not after I'd preached to those young children about the need to follow through on a project, the importance of sticking things out.

With all that turmoil we endured, it is still those young faces I see so clearly, that make me remember the remarkable achievements of a child like Nathan who was hard of hearing and partially blind in one eye. He had a mind that acted like a sponge and his excitement at learning something new was a blessing to behold. He went on to win a state spelling bee.

And I never forget a child like Ruby, who touched me to my soul. When I think of it these many years later, my heart still hurts to remember the pain and lost innocence of that grieving, red haired eight-year-old girl.

Mama's Cat Lies Dying

My mother's cat is in the bathroom, dying. He picked her from a line of humans filing past the cat cages at the animal shelter. She'd gone to get a dog. The cat, a young calico kitten, reached out his paw through the wire grid and slapped at her. His cage mate lay curled beside him, uncommitted. "What was I to do but take him home?" Mama said. "He chose me from all the others."

He was *not* happy with the name she gave him. He wouldn't answer. She thought and searched her heart for a new name. Finally, when she called him Kitty Boy, he came. He's been with her for fifteen years and now he's lying on his soft mat in a corner of the bathroom by the tub. It's where he's liked to hide out in the past, where he could sleep and not be bothered.

He won't take food or water. He's too weak, too exhausted to reach for the saucer of milk, his favorite. "He's not in pain," Mama says, "or I'd whisk him off to the vet. He's just an old kitty whose time has come."

Mama gently held him to her and moved him on his pad to the library while she cleaned the bathroom today. She says she's concerned about his comfort. Perhaps he would rest better, die more easily, if the window panes were polished and the black and white tile mopped. "Anything to help him on his way," she said.

While Mama was busy cleaning, Kitty Boy used the last of his strength to quietly escape, creeping away on fragile legs to her bedroom. He lay there, on the cool bare floor next to her bed. She called his name but he was too weak to answer. When she found him, she carried him back to his dying room. He made no sound and didn't resist. Mama was weeping all the way. "He is so thin and brittle," she cried. It's hard for her to let him go.

She says his dying is a reminder of all those who have left her in the past . . . a husband, her parents, children and friends, a favorite aunt, grandparents, beloved dogs, another favorite cat. "Some dear soul is always leaving."

She sits with him a while, lightly stroking his small gray head, singing the only soothing lullaby she can think of, "Hush, little baby, don't say a word . . ." I watch from the doorway and think that I must remember this song.

Mama has a picture of a young Kitty Boy balancing on the top of the open door to her parents' porch; an impossible leap, but there he is. Mama's parents are gone now, as are the porch and door. Soon Kitty will be gone as well. But Mama has the picture. "I'll frame it and put it on the shelf over my desk," she says. "I'll put it with all the others."

THE SILENCE OF MRS. LAMB

I recall what my mom said just before the screen door slammed and Ronnie came wheeling in from the yard, breaking the mood and filling the house with his angry cries.

"I can't go on like this anymore, Lilly. The pain of losing is too great. How can I be expected to spend the next umpteen years of my life without love?"

She sighed and stood up from the arm of the chair where she had perched, staring out the front window like someone in a dream, having made her pronouncement without looking in my direction, although she had absentmindedly addressed me with words that shook me to my core.

And then things went back to normal.

Ronnie was hollering about the boys in the street who had knocked him off his bike and threatened again to steal it. He was eleven and always yelling about something.

Mom had been blue or depressed or just plain unhappy for so long that I had gotten used to it. I assumed that she had too. I hated Ronnie at this moment. Just as she was about to confide in me for the first time ever, he had to come along and ruin it with his loud mouth and heathen ways.

I screamed back, "Just shut up, Ronnie! You're always in a fight with somebody. Can't you see Mom's upset? We were talking, you nitwit!"

Mom snapped to and looked at me as if seeing me for the first time. "Lilly! Ronnie's just been harangued again by those nasty boys and all you can do is scold him. Let's have a little compassion. Okay?"

I nearly dropped my jaw along with rolling my eyes back into the nether regions of my skull but knew Mom would think I was acting smart. Maybe she didn't realize she had spoken out loud, but she had. There was no mistaking what I'd heard.

I remembered very well the day Daddy left. It was soon after Ronnie turned two, so it has been nine years. I was six. That wasn't the lost love Mom was referring to, however. A few years after the divorce, she met a younger man at the video store.

Jackson was in front of her, holding the Star Wars Trilogy, as she waited to check out movies for us kids. He started up a conversation about his own childhood favorites then waited for Mom outside on the sidewalk. He invited her for a latte at the Starbucks next door.

At first, Mom was shy with Jackson and nervous about seeing him, but he soon got under her skin with his silky voice and bedroom eyes and she was done for. They were obviously crazy about each other. Ronnie and I both thought we were going to end up with this cool, cute stepfather. We secretly compared him to Ashton Kutcher and wished he was as rich. Things swam along for about three years and looked permanent from where we stood. We were young, so what did we know?

Ronnie and I both liked Jackson, despite, or perhaps because he was eight years younger than Mom and always took our side when it seemed important to us. Like the time when we wanted to hang out at the mall for no reason at all and Mom thought it was dangerous or, at the least, a waste of time. Jackson said, "Now Mrs. Lamb," (he jokingly called her by our last name when he wanted to tease), "let's let the kiddies have their fun. No harm in just hanging out." Then he smiled that smile and Mom laughed and we knew we had won again.

One afternoon, I got home late after choir practice. Mom was sitting in that same chair in the living room, holding herself, rocking to and fro. Ronnie was squatted on the floor near her, just watching, with a desperate look in his eyes that even I had to pity.

"What is it, Mom? Are you sick? Does something hurt?" She was silent, but kept on rocking. I threw my books onto the floor. "Ronnie," I said, in my kindest big sister voice, "why don't you get Mom a glass of water. She needs something to wet her whistle. Then you can go out. She's had a rough day and doesn't feel like talking right now."

I used words Mom might have used, but there was no reassurance behind them. I was as bewildered and frightened as Ronnie. I was fifteen, wanting to be an adult, but on my own terms. I did not want to have to take care of Mom as well as my brother.

I set the glass of water on an ugly red plastic coaster on the end table. When Ronnie was out the door, I knelt in front of Mom and took her hands. "Please, Mom, tell me what's wrong." I don't know how long we sat like that, but my fingers grew numb and my knees burned.

With silent tears streaming, she eventually whispered words I nearly missed, "He's gone."

With this, she changed her pattern and began a soft silent rocking side to side, all the while holding herself as if that was all that was keeping her insides from falling out.

Perhaps it was.

I didn't have to ask who and I didn't dare ask why. "Let's go upstairs," I said. "Here, I'll help you."

I offered her the water. She took a sip from the sweating glass, the ice long melted, then allowed me to guide her up to bed. When Ronnie came in, he didn't mention what had happened. I figured he was happy not knowing anything and glad we got to order pizza on a school night. I was feeling superior and self-important, imagining this was the way adults must feel, being in charge of their lives and getting to boss people around. When I got in bed, however, I began to feel like the girl I was, scared and worried about what was coming next.

The next morning, all was as usual. It seemed I had worried for nothing. There was no mention of the previous night. Bless Ronnie, for once. He had the good sense to ask me, not Mom, what had happened to Jackson. When I told him we might never know, he said, "Well, that sucks!"

In the two years following the breakup, Mom never said another word about Jackson until that afternoon a few months back when she perched on the arm of the chair and spoke offhandedly to me.

Coincidentally, about two weeks after she broke her silence on the subject, I ran into Jackson at the theater complex. As far as I knew, it was the first time any of us had seen him since he dumped Mom. I had just come out of my movie when he crossed the lobby to buy popcorn. He was with a college-age girl who had long blonde hair that swung as she walked. I thought of Mom swaying side to side the afternoon I held her. I couldn't see the girl's face. I took pleasure in imagining she had a large, ugly nose.

As they stood at the counter, Jackson put his arm around her waist, turning toward her with that smile I knew so well. As she walked off toward the ladies room, he looked back and saw me.

He smiled again and ambled in my direction. "Lilly, hey. What a surprise. How you doin'?"

I stared at him, thinking I would speak, expecting that we would have an awkward conversation, that I might even have to say a word or two to the blonde when she came out of the bathroom. But I am my mother's child. I stood and stared and said nothing, not one blamed thing.

Jackson frowned and eventually said, "Well, gotta go. Tell Maggie and Ronnie I said hi."

I think it was hearing him call Mom by name that did it. To

his departing back, making my words count, I said, "In a rat's ass, you scumbag!"

He stopped, took a deep breath, nodded, and walked on.

I've never told Ronnie or Mom about running into Jackson, but when I got home that day, I went straight to the kitchen and gave Mom a big hug. "Hey, what's that for?"

"Just that we love you, Mom. Ronnie and I love you. We always will."

She stood back and took a long look at me, tears welling. "And I you, my darling girl," she said. "And I, you."

Do It Now . . . Or Wait and See

It made sense for me to be the one to clear out the house. Sissy lives in Denver and Daniel in St. Paul. Daddy died of Parkinson's twelve years ago. I'm the one who lives—who lived—near Mama in Selma. Still, it took me three weeks and six days to get the job done.

I hired Mattie from the church to come afternoons when she finished at the Rectory, to help box up stuff and clean as we went. My neighbor's grandson came by to help with the heavy lifting. I could have finished much sooner, but I wanted time to go through the attic, Mama's closet, her desk. I spent one whole day just looking at photographs. I smiled some, laughed a little, and cried a whole lot.

Mama had a great library filled with all sorts of books. There were some classics. . . . she loved Austen and the Brontes. She had romance novels from the fifties and experimental plays from the seventies. Mama liked a little bit of everything, as long as it was in print. She liked the feel of a book, she said, and although she thought words were sacred, she had no problem curling up in bed or on the couch, eating and drinking as she read, smudging the pages with grease spots and chocolate. *Gone With the Wind* and the complete works of O'Henry were badly stained. I couldn't bear to part with a single one. I bought extra shelves at Ikea that now fill an entire wall in my living room.

Knowing how Mama liked to save things, I knew I would find notes and letters and cards she kept. What I never expected was to find a box of poems Mama had penned when she was perhaps twelve or thirteen. And there was a stack of essays, all written before she was forty. Reading them one by one was like opening an Advent calendar with its bright little windows, each revealing a message or a gift.

Beyond herself, which she shared with us freely when she was alive, her writing is the greatest gift she could have left for us. Over a period of days, I read everything, sitting alone on her back screen porch, empty of all but the dark green wicker chair I had left until last. I took my time, sipping my coffee or iced tea from Mama's favorite "Life is a Beach" mug, while savoring her words.

Since cleaning out the house last year and putting it up for sale after Goodwill made their final pickup, I've wanted to write a piece about Mama, something to honor her memory. But I realized that to best describe her depth and worth to me, to really define who she was, I could do no better than to share something she wrote. I think her final essay might say it best.

◡

DO IT NOW, OR WAIT AND SEE

This, my dears, is one of the great dilemmas in life: knowing when to act now, and when to put a thing off until later, or perhaps never. Choosing wisely can make your life easier, more loving, more peaceful, and even more fun, and there are times when knowing how to choose can save a life, a friendship, a marriage. It is no small thing. Just as with life, time is a gift from God.

But how do you decide? Sometimes the choice seems obvious. Wait and see if the leg cramp goes away. Hang out for another fifteen minutes; they're probably just running late. Forget what the directions say, pull the rolls out of the oven right-this-minute or they'll be too charred to eat.

But it's not always that simple. How serious is the baby's fever, or your son's headaches, or that strange little mole you've noticed for the first time? And the argument with your friend? It seems silly to you now, but was she hurt by your frankness?

I don't know the answers—wish I did, but here are a few guidelines.

If the pain is horrific, go now . . . to the doctor, the ER. Don't wait. If the fever doesn't break, same advice. Same thing applies to blurry vision, mental confusion, other signs of stroke or heart attack, choking and excessive bleeding, no matter where it's coming from. And snake bites? Get help regardless of the fact that you have the merit badge!

And when you have the opportunity, or the opportunity to *make* the opportunity, tell them—your family and your friends— that you love them, think they're great, will support them, and that you wish them well. Forgive them for anything and everything and leave the judgments to God. Brag on folks for who they are and what they've done. And don't give up the chance to compliment someone on something specific. Anything will do, although if you know what will please them the most, then name that first.

Whenever there's any doubt, serious doubt, best to leave things unsaid or undone. Hold your tongue, even if it chokes you. No need to wheel off into eternity with your bitter words whirling about the universe. They might just catch up with you in the next world and bite you where it hurts.

Save the anger, the meanness, for the letter you write but never send, the note you rip to shreds and flush. Or take that anger to a tree deep in the woods. Use it as your sounding board. Stand in front of that tree and scream at it 'til you're blue, shouting obscenities and muttering curses which will never be heard by human ears. It might scare a squirrel or cause a rabbit to run, but no matter. It won't break a heart, even your own, or cost you the love and trust of someone you hold dear.

⤳

I have to believe that Mama wrote this with us in mind, knowing we would find it one day. It's all good advice, just platitudinous, the way good advice often is. Reading it again, I wonder about those years she nursed Daddy. Did she wish she had been kinder, more understanding of his horrific situation? Perhaps she had wanted him to show more appreciation for all that she did for him, for the sacrifices she made in her life to accommodate his. Maybe both. Maybe neither.

I know I still feel guilty that I wasn't around more during those years to help them both. Even being away at school seems a poor excuse from this distance. Sissy was just married and having babies, and Daniel had just started a new job. Toward the end, when things got bad, I could have dropped out for a year or two and gone back later. They would have made a fuss, but even so, I will always think that's what I should have done.

Perhaps this is simply what it seems on the surface: our loving mother's letter to her children, helpful words to guide us through our lives without her reminders of how to be in a world where she will no longer be at hand to urge or nudge, admonish or protect, and to love and praise us as she did in life. I hate to think it is anything more. Mama had no reason for guilty regrets. She did what she was called upon to do in her life and her marriage and handled it all with grace and a lot of class. I could do no better than to follow her example.

The One Big Question

Daddy is the one who found her in the garage, slumped over in the front seat of her car with a pink polka-dot shower cap covering her face like a death mask, oxygen-deprived as she drifted into eternity with the help of a number of over-the-counter sleep aids.

There was no note. That was what the police determined and what we were given to face. Mama had taken her own life and left us—her distraught, stunned, and grieving family—with nothing in the way of explanation.

If she had been seeing a therapist or a doctor, we were not aware of it. Our small town police checked around and said they found no appointments scheduled. Our minister said no, no recent visits to him that might have helped to explain her "obvious state of mind," as the coroner's office put it. There were no last-minute calls to friends or secret admirers. The police said the phone records of cell and land lines indicated no activity.

So, there we were. With no one to help make sense of it.

I have to say, it has given us all something to focus on: why Mama would leave us in such a way and without so much as a "fare-thee-well, my chickadees." How dare she?

It has been two months. We still have no answers.

Jillian says Daddy spends his days spinning the radio dial and flipping TV channels. She reports he has quit talking and eats very little, that he has aged ten years. We are thankful he still does his daily ablutions so that his personal care has not become our responsibility.

I stayed with him for the first month, but had to get back to my real life. I write him once a week, knowing not to expect an answer. When I call him on Sundays, I am always surprised when he picks up the phone. Once he does, there is so little to talk about.

Our brother, Jonathan, considers himself the cause of Mama's dramatic departure. This is no surprise to Jillian and me. Perhaps because he is the middle child, he has chosen the role of victim time and again throughout his thirty-eight years. How he came to this recent conclusion is a mystery, although we think it is because he saw Mama the least and is eaten up with guilt. I also think he likes wallowing at center stage.

Although she says she doesn't blame herself for Mama's suicide, Jillian wrestles constantly with the loss of her best friend. She is the baby, even at thirty, and lives in the same neighborhood as our parents. She and Mama were close, very close, and saw each other every day. Jillian's heart is broken and there is now a hole in her life that I can hardly comprehend from this distance. I worry about her the most. Still, I am thankful I live three states away.

Jillian thinks I'm angry. She could be right. I do not yet know what I feel. When those around me are in mental pain or grieving, I retreat inward. My emotions clamp down like shuttered windows on an abandoned building. I do not seem to have the power to unlatch those blinds. I go through the days presenting a cheerful façade to the world which seems to make folks happy enough and causes me little discomfort. It is not deliberate and whether it is a sign of cowardice or a healthy psyche, I cannot say. It is just my way.

So here we are, Daddy and Jonathan, Jillian and me, each of us attempting to come to terms with our loss, trying to get on with our lives as best we can. And yet, for all our hopeful intentions as we struggle forward, now and forever, with no promise of an answer, we will be asking the one big question: "Why, Mama? Why?"

The Prohibitionist's Mother

The other night at a party, I had a mixed drink that tasted so good I could have drunk a pitcherful. The base for the drink is pink lemonade. It's called a "Hop, Skip, and Go Naked." Besides giving me a clue to its potency, the name made me laugh. I was alone and had to drive, so I drank just the one delicious drink and switched to ice water. Not nearly as tasty and offering no promise of things to come.

My sister said she used to drink something called a "Pink Pull-Your-Panties-Down" which I'm told is the same thing as a "Panties Dropper." Probably not wise to try one of those in mixed company!

All of this reminded me that there was a time before I was old enough to imbibe that I was a crusader against the devil drink, a child prohibitionist.

My parents drank beer, nothing else that I'm aware of besides cold bottled Pabst Blue Ribbon. Do they even make that anymore?

My father, who had been raised in a teetotaling household, didn't have a drink until he was in college. He might have tried some of those rotgut concoctions college kids are famous for making, but he settled on beer, price and availability probably being major considerations.

Mama, on the other hand, was left motherless as a young girl and, as an only child, became her pa's best companion. She learned to drink at home when she was old enough to play poker and a game called "You're Snooked." She and her pa played cards and drank beer and ate curly salted pretzels.

Unlike some neighbors who reportedly piled their empty wooden beer crates high in a corner of their living room by the front door, my parents were discreet. They bought their beer one six pack at a time. They drank only on the weekend and only at night and very little at that. So it was not flamboyant drunkenness that prompted my crusade. It was the church.

When I was twelve, we moved to a house out from town, nearly in the country. It was two doors away from a small church that depended on visiting ministers and revivals to keep up the enthusiasm of the limited congregation. It was during one of these radical revivals that I "got saved," "saw the Light," and set out to change the world, beginning at home. Temperance became my cause.

In my defense, the preacher did magic tricks up front, with clear pitchers of water and something that turned one of them red as blood and back again, serving to demonstrate the need for cleansing ourselves of the evils of the world. It was powerful stuff he preached.

I was too young for sex and didn't have a boyfriend at the time, so what else was I to do with all those raging hormones? Channeling that adolescent energy for good, I began to proselytize and weep. It frightened my father who had no idea that girls could get so crazy and still be sane. Mama just sat and listened to me, nodded appropriately, and continued what she was doing as if nothing had been said which could possibly change her mind. She had recently learned to eat pizza and she wasn't giving up her accompanying beverage of choice without a fight.

My parents never left my little sister and me alone to go anywhere. One evening not long after my conversion, we all went to a party. Mama put my sister to bed in the guestroom. I was left to entertain myself while the grownups partied.

As the evening wore on, I curled up on a couch and fell asleep. I was awakened by loud music and laughter. I went looking for

Mama and Daddy through the dancing crowd.

I was horrified to find my mother sitting in a basket on the floor with a lampshade on her head. Everyone was laughing to beat the band and having a perfectly marvelous time. I stood staring sleepy-eyed at this unbelievable scene and openly pled with Daddy to take us home. I was tired and wanted out of what the preacher would call a den of iniquity (although I wasn't certain of the meaning, I recognized iniquity when I saw it).

The next day was Sunday. My parents, who rarely went to church anyway, were definitely not going on this day. They didn't look so hot and obviously didn't feel so good either. Things were quiet at our house that morning.

Being newly saved and full of arrogant piety, I pranced off across the yards to church to refill myself with strength of purpose.

That afternoon, inspired by another fiery sermon, I worked myself into a frenzy and pled with my parents, great tears and all, to quit drinking. Daddy got nervous and left the room. Mama watched me calmly, but there must have been growing alarm when I hit my stride and began to beg in earnest. "Please, Mama, I don't want you and Daddy to burn in Hell!"

Two nights later, Mama made the announcement. She and Daddy had talked it over and come to a decision. They had heard my cries and been touched. No more alcohol. They were giving it up for good. No more beer in the house for me to be ashamed of, no more beer with pizza to throw me into fits. Right had triumphed and I was able to go off full of pride and satisfaction, knowing I had won a battle for Jesus. Singlehandedly, I had saved my parents from the threat of Hell's fire and Everlasting Damnation.

Years later, after the boyfriends, after sex, after I was married, and after I had definitely become a backslider, I took up drinking myself. I found out firsthand what all the to-do was about and I liked it. There were Pink Squirrels and Brandy Alexanders which went down oh so nicely. It was the seventies and there were more opportunities to drink than ever. I learned to toss back a martini like Bond, shaken, not stirred, and I learned which drink fit which occasion.

Once in a while when the thought crossed my mind, I felt a little guilty that I had been instrumental in causing my folks to give up their innocent and occasional beers. I was amazed to think my hysterics had wielded such influence. But I never said anything to them about it.

At a holiday brunch we were having, I served bloody Marys and mimosas, perfect midmorning concoctions. My parents stopped by for a few minutes and I found myself alone in the kitchen with my mother. I was ruffling around, putting things on platters and pulling dishes out of the oven, being very busy, and feeling overly important as the hostess.

I reached for my bloody Mary on the counter where it was watering down from the kitchen heat and took a large gulp. "You need to have one of these," I said to Mama. "They are sooooo good."

"No, thank you, honey. I don't believe I will," she said, putting her hand on my arm. "Surely, you must remember that your daddy and I don't drink. We wish you'd give it up too, sweetie. I hope you'll seriously consider it. We don't want to be separated from you in the afterlife. It grieves us to think that while we're rejoicing with Jesus in Beulah Land, you could be burning in the everlasting fires of Hell."

I took a platter of hot biscuits to the dining room table and, on my way, I whispered to my husband, "Honey, would you please pour me a fresh bloody Mary? I seem to have misplaced mine."

THE GRADUATE

When my mother turned sixty, I was afraid she would begin to wear ecclesiastical purple, joining the red hat/purple outfit group of women who celebrate their age by acting like embarrassingly silly little girls in dress-up. The When-I-Am-Old-I-Will-Wear-Purple poem had circulated through Mom's group of friends. A couple of them took it seriously. It sounded exactly like something she would endorse.

As it turned out, that might have been preferable to what she actually did.

She went back to school and, depending on the season, dressed in Bermuda shorts and sandals or plaid skirts with tights and loafers.

After the first year, she modernized her wardrobe to something even more ridiculous but in keeping with what the other sophomores were wearing: short, bare, revealing, mismatched see-through get-ups with frightening shoes and expensive handbags. I suspect my mother's was the only one that held a prescription for hormones and an extra pair of bifocals. I particularly hated the colored bras and straps that showed through every outfit she wore.

One expects that a parent might become a little dotty with the encroaching years, like filling the house with cats or piling up old copies of *The National Observer* in a corner of the bedroom, but not that they would deliberately *choose* embarrassing behavior! Early on, my brother, who is good at avoiding everything distasteful, just laughed and pretended it was life as usual. I, on the other hand, spent a lot of time in the shower crying. That's the best place to cry, by the way. It's so private, and running water muffles the sound of wailing.

When she was a junior, my mother Lizzie (no longer Elizabeth), spent the summer backpacking in Europe with a group of her young study buddies and took courses at Oxford where, I'm led to believe by some of the gossip that followed, she carried on a short but torrid affair with one of her dons.

Dear God, is nothing sacred?

I thought the English were prim and proper and barely approachable, their universities overrun with homosexual intellectuals.

There's another of my illusions gone bust.

Even though they were long divorced, I thanked heaven that Daddy was dead. Had he not been, all this would have killed him for sure.

Unlike me, who knows how to dress my age and majored in Education with a minor in Business, something actually *useful,* Mom is getting her degree this spring with a major in Asian Culture and a minor in Psychology.

To be honest, I never thought she'd get this far and I recognize that four years of college at her age is a real feat. I am trying to feel proud and happy for her. I must admit, however, that I'm concerned about what comes next. It remains to be seen what she can do with her strange degree.

Mostly though, I just pray she doesn't further embarrass us at graduation by wearing a red mortarboard and purple hightops.

Romancing the Public

Emily Douglas Brewton, the romance writer, is my mother. Perhaps you have read one or more of her books. They can be found with similar paperbacks at the grocery.

You know the ones.

The covers show a handsome, roguish fellow on horseback, attempting the rescue of a lovely, raven-haired, bodice-ripped damsel, or something equally unlikely and romantic.

While the covers and titles may change slightly, the stories within are formulaic. It is difficult for me to maintain interest in a book with such a predictable outcome. Fortunately for my mother, there are millions of readers who don't seem to be put off by this point.

I am often approached by people who ask me about her and request that I pass along their comments on her work. Usually their remarks are favorable, even effusive, generally put to me by highly excited matrons, but I have listened to a couple of rather severe critiques which I chose to keep to myself. My mother would not necessarily be surprised or shocked by the criticism. She would, however, take up too much of my time with questions about why anyone could have major concerns about a romance novel.

"After all, Marianne, they are not serious books by any stretch of the imagination," she once said. "How people can get so wrapped up in such nonsense is beyond me. Don't they understand entertainment for entertainment's sake?"

I must give my mother credit for this realistic insight. She may be a great romantic, but she's not stupid.

Although I am frequently accosted by her fans, I still find it hard to comprehend that she has become something of a celebrity, as well as a self-made millionaire, considering it all began at our kitchen table fourteen years ago.

I was in high school at the time and had come in from a movie to find Mom hunched over a yellow writing tablet, feverishly at work. I gave her a goodnight kiss and stopped long enough to look over her shoulder. "What's up?"

"I'm venting, Marianne. I hate your father and his unromantic spirit, so I'm venting. I'll make my own romance. Just you wait and see!" She went back to her furious scribbling.

And that's exactly how it started. Evidently, my mother wasn't feeling fulfilled and she decided to take it out on Daddy with the written word. She has always been a fool for the romantic. As a long-time consumer of the romance genre, she believed it would be easy to replicate. And so it was. But surely only someone with my mother's romantic disappointments and driving anger could have done it so well.

Although she is still a romantic, she is probably less so now that she is surrounded by so much drivel and has had to exercise the other side of her brain with business dealings. Her fantasies are still alive and well, however, or she couldn't continue to pump out these books at the rate she does.

I have to credit David, also. He is Mom's new and younger husband, perfect for the situation in which she finds herself.

He is her helpmate in the truest sense of the word. He handles her travel plans, arranges for autograph sessions, keeps her appointment schedule, gets her where she needs to be at the right time (no mean feat with my mother, who is always late) and treats her in the most loving ways.

Of course, it takes a man with a certain disposition and a willingness to forego any particular plans of his own. I'm certain the task is made easier for David who is being cared for by a spouse who gives him freedom with her generous income. In any case, they have evidently met some balance which pleases them both.

I frequently see my father and his wife, Adele, and my step-sister, Adrian, who is seven. They live in Manhattan and I think nothing of scooting up there once or twice a month from my little hamlet in northern Virginia where I teach mathematics in a small private school. It's a short flight and I love having a reason to stay with this happy family in such an exhilarating town. It's a way I help make up to myself for the sort of family life I yearned for as an only child when I felt so lonely.

Adele and my father seem to truly adore each other and my stepsister is both the baby sister I always wanted and the daughter I will never have. As much as I love sharing his new life, it is hard to see my father so happy with someone else. If only it could have been my mother.

I haven't come out to my family yet, but I'll get around to tell-ing them when, if, I ever run into anyone I want to get serious about. So far, my career is going well and I haven't felt the need to encumber myself with a life partner.

I know Adele will be supportive (I'm certain she already sus-pects), and Daddy will probably say nothing, out of confusion and embarrassment. My mother, on the other hand, could go either way. She may cry and blame herself, wringing her hands over the fact that I'm not the daughter she had hoped for, but I don't think so. Most likely, she will take the stance that as long as there's "ro-mance" in my life, more's the power.

It is a little known fact that the villains and protagonists in each of Mom's twenty-seven published books have been named for friends and family members. I, Marianne, was the blonde damsel in *Waves Across the Delta*. My father, John, was the dashing hero in *Hearts Under a Blood Moon*. That was book number two which gave me hope that all would be well with their marriage . . . wishful thinking on the part of a teenage girl.

According to my mother, there was never any hope for them after the night I found her writing those first pages of *Long Forgotten Love in Carolina*. Daddy has had the poor taste to suggest that his lack of concern for my mother's needs (I certainly haven't questioned what *those* might have been) is what helped to make her a self-sufficient, rich divorcee.

I once asked her why she had never used her own name in one of her novels. "Oh, Emily is much too timid for a dramatic heroine. It's not even a good name for someone who writes passionate literature, excepting Emily Dickinson, of course. If I weren't so well established, I believe I'd change it to something that evokes drama and sounds far more exotic."

I have just finished the first-draft reading of her newest novel, *Love Songs Under a New Sky*. I note with interest that the hero, David, named for her present husband, is more sensitive and reliable than Edward, the dark and brooding villainous first love of our heroine who bears my father's middle name. And at long last, my mother may have very well used poetic license to its best advantage and given us a rose-colored glimpse of her fantasy self.

I believe this newest volume is her best yet and that the public will request—no, demand—a sequel for our industrious, mysterious, and beautiful heroine, the enchanting and captivating India. I smile when I see this well-chosen suitably romantic name and acknowledge that not even I can argue with such success.

BLINDED BY THE LIGHT

"Nothing has ever been right." These were words my mother uttered again and again. When we were young, my brothers and sister and I tried our best to change her thinking. We assumed that it must have something to do with us, must somehow be *our* fault that things had never been right.

"Oh, Mama, please don't say that," we would chorus, then begin our litany of gifts, of blessings that we saw so clearly, even at our young ages. "You've got *us,* Mama, and you've got Daddy, and *that's* right . . . and you got to be in that beauty thing at school, you said, and you got that job you wanted that time, and . . ."

When we were a little older, but young enough that she still had our attention, she told us she had always been the wrong age for anything good—either too young or too old.

She believed she had been single when she should have married, married when she would have done well to be single; living alone when she should have had a roommate, sharing quarters with someone when being by herself would have made all the difference; and so on.

By the time we were teenagers, when she was able to catch the boys' fleeting notice, they would listen to her with an irritated tolerance and a, "Right, Mom." My sister, Janet, and I turned deaf ears to anything either of our parents had to say. If we bothered to notice at all, we just rolled our eyes at each other but said nothing. None of us had ever been able to determine the source of Mama's complaints. From where we sat, she had a pretty good, though not particularly exciting, life.

At some point, I realized that Mama never made any of these comments when Daddy was around. Did she never say these things to him? In the privacy of their room or perhaps in the car on their way to a party, might she not have blurted out her ongoing disappointments? But Daddy has never given any indication he was aware of what must have been a deep discontentment on her part.

How could that even be possible?

I say that, but know that I am guilty of the same sort of withholding from my husband. Why start something that will probably be misunderstood and end unhappily for us both?

About six years ago, Mama and I were coming back from a trip to see Janet's new apartment in Raleigh where she had taken a job teaching speech- and hearing-impaired children. We had spent the night on two musty, lumpy rollouts Janet had borrowed for our visit, and were glad to be up and going home to our own beds a hundred miles away.

We stopped for breakfast on the road. As we waited in the restaurant booth for our food, we looked out the rain-streaked window onto a wet gray day. Across from our vintage pancake house was a red brick fundamentalist church with a blinking road-side sign proclaiming: *Like Paul, YOU must be Blinded by the Light.*

Mama read it aloud slowly, repeating the message several times in a barely audible mumble.

"I'm guessing they mean *St.* Paul," I said, staring at the flashing sign. "His epiphany. Right?" One of the few stories I remembered from vacation bible school. I turned to face Mama across the scarred wooden table that smelled of layers of old grease and Clorox.

I saw her expression change. It was as if some invisible veil was lifting. What I would describe as a slow, sweet smile of discernment began to spread across her face. In that instant, I witnessed something miraculous, unexplainable, yet sublime. Mama's hazel eyes shone with a new light when she looked at me directly. "That's it, Sharon. That's the answer—what I've been searching for!"

For a moment, I was stunned into silence. Then, knowing she probably couldn't answer the question, I asked it anyway. "What? What's been missing?"

With a barely perceptible shrug, she whispered, "God . . ."

I wasn't sure I had heard her.

With a tentative smile, she added, "Simply my dependence on God."

I slowly nodded. Sitting across from me in this old, ordinary pancake house in North Carolina, my mother had been blessed with some sort of beatific experience.

I couldn't think of anything more to say. The waitress appeared with our pancakes and sausage. We ate in silence. Preoccupied with trying to decipher what had just happened, I looked around at the other diners. They were unmoved by what was going on at our table. Mama glanced out the window occasionally, then down at her plate. I still don't know why I found it so unsettling. Perhaps because religion, like sex, was never discussed at home. It made us all uneasy. I was relieved when no mention of her "enlightenment" was made during the remainder of our ride home.

Shortly after that trip, I moved to Sarasota to work at the Ringling, delighted to be using my art history degree. I never again had much day-to-day contact with either of my parents. I can't say whether anything specific changed in my mother's life because of her roadside epiphany. I do know I never again heard her complain about things not being right. When we did get together, she seemed much the same as always, though more content or cheerful, and with a softer edge. I don't know about my brothers, but Janet noticed it, too. She thought it was because Mama had started going to the Methodist church. "Maybe the preacher's gotten hold of her," she joked.

On a visit home, I saw that Mama had a scripture verse from

Acts pushed into the corner of her dresser mirror. It recounted the conversion of St. Paul on the road to Damascus. I had never told anyone about the pancake house episode. It had been a preternatural experience, and because I couldn't explain it, I wanted to put it out of my mind. Until recently.

Last August, while driving to town late one afternoon, Mama was killed in a single car accident. People at the scene said they thought it was caused by the glare from the setting sun. We found her sunglasses at home, forgotten on the hall table.

Apparently, as she headed west, squinting against a stream of oncoming traffic, the sun, lying in wait near the horizon, cast one last brilliant explosion of light as it tipped to the other side of the world, taking Mama with it as she lost control of her car and went crashing headlong into eternity in that final, exquisite blinding moment of her life.

WANDERING JEW

I was nine years old when my mother left. I came home from school one afternoon and she was gone. No letter, not even for me. Nothing.

It was more than ten years before I saw her again. No one could—or would—explain why she had gone or where.

"She just left," my grandmother said, "while I was at the A&P. She packed her stuff and was gone when I got back."

"I'm sorry, Christie. I just don't know," my father said.

That wasn't good enough for me. It was hard to believe either of them. One thing I did know, even as young as I was: she hadn't deserted us because of me. Her leaving had to be a part of something larger, something I could not yet understand. Otherwise, she would have told me. She told me everything. At least, I thought she had told me everything. As it turned out, she had told me nothing.

As a child, before I was jaded by the awful truths of the world, I believed that a mother who loves you at night, who sings lullabies and reads bedtime stories would never, in the light of the following day, leave because of her child. It would always be something else that took her away. It was this notion, that I was not responsible, that got me past blaming myself. Unfortunately, it didn't keep me from blaming others. It never occurred to me to blame my Mama.

Gran Lowe tried, in her own sweet way, to console me. She hugged me a lot, pulling me to her at every chance, making up little errands for me to run, asking for help while she cooked, making my favorite desserts. She left my bedroom door cracked at night with the hall light on and talked Daddy into letting me go to the movies twice on the weekends. I wasn't made to go to Sunday school or church for a month. Even with the distractions, I missed Mama.

I could only guess at what effect her leaving had on Daddy and Gran since they didn't talk about it. It went unsaid, but I understood that I wasn't to mention Mama or her going. When he was home, Daddy mostly kept to himself. He spent a lot of time just staring into space. I knew it was a space that held my mother.

Gran continued to keep house for us and Daddy went off to his paint store every day, just like before. My school friends and the ladies at church looked on me with pity for a short while and then they were done. . . . nothing to make me think that anyone even remembered the most important event in my life. It seemed that I alone suffered the pain of her leaving. And I alone would cope with my grief.

My best friend, Molly Hodge, was the only one I confided in. But even that was minimal. Molly was good, not a lot of questions and she listened well, but I saw soon enough that no one could help me, not really. No one else could possibly understand. I was the only girl any of us knew who had been abandoned by her mother. I can tell you that you never get over that.

I cried myself to sleep at night for exactly one year. By then, I was tired of waking up every morning with a dull headache and I was afraid the weeping would eventually ruin my nose. More importantly, it hadn't brought Mama back. So I stopped.

Mama sent me a few cards over the years, but never when one might have expected. No birthday cards, no Christmas or Easter greetings, just random cards with pleasant sentiments. "Thinking of You" was a favorite. I got a bulletin board for my room and painted the frame pink to match the flowers on my bedspread. I tacked up the cards so that I could be reminded that my mother still thought of me. The cards were never enough nor what I hoped for, but I reasoned that if she wrote at all, she must miss me. Obviously, not enough to bring her back home. She always signed them, Your Mama. At least she remembered *that* much.

Everything was postmarked Washington state, but not because Mama was there. She sent them to her sister in Seattle who would mail them for her. I didn't know this at the time, so I grew up believing she lived in the Northwest. It was there where my mind wandered, my fantasies set adrift.

While I lived in the small Georgia town, being raised by my quiet, handsome father and my grandmother, I dreamed of life in a cooler, wet climate. I asked for an atlas so I could chart the distance between us, my mother and me. I checked out books from the library about sailboats, the coastline of the western United States, lumberjacking.

Mama's family was never mentioned either. Once, when I was insistent, Gran reminded me that my mother and her sister had lived in an orphanage until Mama was old enough to take a job. She and Daddy had met in New Jersey when he was in the Army and stationed at Camp Kilmer. Mama was working behind the counter at the local coffee shop. When they were married and his tour was up, they came south to live in his hometown.

I had known there was a sister because they stood side by side in the only photograph I had of Mama as a young girl. Her brown eyes peered from behind long, dark bangs while her little sister appeared to have lighter hair and eyes. This was mainly supposition. The picture had been taken from such a distance that details were difficult to make out. What is certain is that I, a lanky blonde with blue eyes, take after my father's family of German extraction. People say that Pete Lowe could have spit me out. I'd have given anything to trade for my mother's dark beauty.

In sixth grade, my English teacher read to us from the *Diary of Anne Frank* in an effort to encourage us to keep diaries of our own. Seeing the cover picture, I became convinced that my mother was Jewish because of her childhood resemblance to the thin little Anne. I was captured by the words of the young girl and strongly affected by the feelings they inspired. I spent my allowance on a copy of the book to keep beside my bed.

I came to believe that my father had married my mother without knowledge of her heritage. When he found out years later, he could not tolerate her Jewishness and drove her from our home. Convinced of this, I took a dislike to my father and grandmother for what I believed they must have perpetrated on my sweet, innocent mother. I was obsessed with this notion. I withdrew from Gran and treated Daddy with contempt. They may have assumed my behavior was age-related since it is well-documented that hormonal girls from twelve to eighteen can be strange and volatile creatures.

One night at supper, my fantasies got the best of me. We were having pan-fried catfish and cheese grits with Gran's delicious slaw and hushpuppies. I remember that it was a pleasant evening with windows open and a light breeze. Despite the casual menu, Gran had me set the table with her floral Rosalinde china and the good silver. It was that kind of weather.

After Daddy said the blessing and filled his plate, I spoke up, demanding he explain why my Jewish mother hadn't been good enough for us. "How could you do that? How could you run her off?" I asked. "What did she ever do to you?"

With a look of dumbfounded shock, Daddy laid his fork down beside his plate and stared at me across the length of the damask-covered dining table. The only sound was Gran's tiny gasp.

He did not immediately answer, but stared down the table with a look I had never seen. Go to your room," he said. "Now." His clinched jaw was twitching.

I opened my mouth to speak, but decided against it. This was not the time. I went up to bed and tucked Anne's diary under my pillow.

At breakfast the next morning, Daddy walked in and stood behind me. I could smell the Lilac Vegetal and I felt his large hands grasp the back of my chair. I was having oatmeal, hot and sticky sweet with sugar and melting butter. Having missed my dinner the night before, I was starving. But I waited, holding my spoon away from the bowl until he spoke.

"I cannot imagine where you got such a notion, Christie, but I can assure you this: your mother is not now and never was a Jew. And had she been, it would not have mattered one whit. And she did *not* leave this house because she was mistreated. You will have to take my word on this."

The manner in which he spoke left me with no doubts. I knew he was telling the truth. "Yes, sir," I said.

I wanted to say that none of this would have happened if they had only told me the truth about her going. But I thought better of it and kept my mouth shut except to eat.

That afternoon, I donated my copy of the diary to the school library with a note to my teacher suggesting she might want to re-think recommending that book. Without elaborating, I told her it had gotten me into a whole lot of trouble.

I thought a lot about the weather during the early years, wondering if Mama liked rain and fog and cloudy, gray days. Maybe that was what drove her away and to Seattle; she found our skies too bright. She felt parched and burned and needed relief from our scorching sun and muggy summers. When I was fourteen, I read some Tennessee Williams and learned how women could be affected by the southern heat. Perhaps it had driven Mama to madness or turned her into an alcoholic or worse. I pictured her as beautiful, fragile, a tortured soul. I thought I understood. I know now, that so long as I could romanticize my loss, I couldn't blame her for leaving.

No one volunteered to talk about my mother except for her self-proclaimed best friend, Edna Harper. She took every chance she could find to corner me and state her sympathy. She would chatter on about that close and wonderful time in their lives, but hardly said anything specific about Mama. I didn't recall Mama having any close friends and decided that Miss Edna had made it all up. When I asked Gran, she said "Well now, that's no new trick, trying to get on your good side. Honey, she's just after your daddy." What I was sure of was that this skinny, bleached blond was not my mother's type and certainly not mine. I prayed she wasn't Daddy's type either.

Even though I missed Mama terribly in the beginning, I gradually got used to living with what little family I had left. She was never far from my thoughts, but I fell into a routine that, looking back now, I can see was really pretty normal. After the diary debacle, I gave up fighting and relaxed into a new, happier version of my life.

I did well in school and was popular enough to make cheerleader. Gran had her bridge and garden club. Daddy's business did well and he was able to leave someone else in charge most Saturdays so he could go fishing. I know that he occasionally took a lady to the movie or a dance at the club, but he never once brought anyone home for us to meet. It was my grandmother who told me later that he had waited for five years before he filed for divorce. By then, I had a steady boyfriend and was too involved to care about much else. Good times and John C. were all that mattered.

I graduated from Caulfield High with a B average and planned to go on to college. First, I wanted a summer job, so I went to work for Mr. Soames at the bank. I was treated very well since he and Daddy were friends. He assured me I could go a long way with Southern Community Trust. I liked the sound of it and decided to stay. College could wait.

By then, John C. had been replaced by Tolly Crawford who was a god and unbelievably good to me. Tolly was twenty, had one more year of college, and would eventually become a partner in his family's wholesale food business. His parents and sisters seemed to like me just fine. He and Daddy got along and Gran thought him a real catch. She said that I would be safe with him. Life was good.

When I had been at the bank exactly two years, Tolly proposed and we decided on a wedding in June, six months away. The announcement was in the paper with my picture and a quarter-column about our plans. Family friends sent lovely notes or called to offer congratulations. Molly and I plotted and planned and decided it should be a morning wedding at home in my grandmother's beautiful garden. Gran and her circle of ladies happily stepped in and took charge of arrangements.

Because it will be a morning affair, I've chosen a simple pattern for a dress with a neckline to show off my grandmother's pearls. Molly and Gran and I went to Sampson's to pick out the fabric. We chose a lightweight faille for the lining and stark white organza for the dress. Mrs. Salter is making my dress. I plan to wear miniature gardenias as my hairpiece and will carry a bouquet of white lilies and gardenias wrapped with streamers of narrow white satin ribbon. Molly has given me a lacy blue garter and her mother is lending me her wedding handkerchief. Gran has the women of the church praying for perfect weather. Everything is covered.

Two weeks ago, on Wednesday, the fourth of May, I looked up from my teller's post to help the first customer of the morning. A deeply tanned lady with dark sunglasses and sun-streaked hair approached.

"Good morning. How may I help you?"

She presented a hundred dollar bill and asked for change. I made the transaction and she thanked me. On her way to the door, she handed something to Ted, the security man. She turned and took one look back in my direction, then passed through the heavy brass doors into the bright morning.

"Here you go, Christie, from that lady that just walked out." Ted handed me an envelope.

It was a card with a drawing of a pair of doves on the front and "Congratulation on Your Upcoming Nuptials" in raised silver script. On the inside, the sentiment was written in a familiar hand:

May you both be the happiest you can be
when you are together
And the unhappiest you can be when
you are apart.
Best wishes for a happy life.

Your Mama

I was stunned. When I found my feet, I streaked out to the sidewalk. There were three people in sight, but not the lady with the card. Old Mr. French was parking his car. Otherwise, the street was quiet for a couple of blocks either way.

I told Mr. Soames I wasn't feeling well and had to leave for the day. I called Tolly to come and get me. He took me home and sat with me on the back screen porch, listening patiently as I cried and ranted. I was thankful it was Gran's bridge day out. Tolly sat across from me holding my hands, his back to the screen door.

I looked past him to the garden. The hydrangeas were in bloom, an overwhelming hedge of blue, recently fertilized to keep them healthy and beautiful for the wedding. As long as the days continue sunny, we will have pink roses blooming on either side of the white runner Gran plans to have laid down for my procession from the house. "I don't want you messing up your hem in the early damp," she said. "These roses we planted will complement the bridesmaids' pale pink organza."

When Daddy came in for dinner, I thrust the card at him accusingly. His shoulders visibly drooped as I presented him with another of my unexpected bombshells. He looked at the card slowly, front and back, then settled on the written verse. He took a while to speak.

"She couldn't stay still," he said. "She was restless after we came back here. It was just a part of who she was. She had to wander and I couldn't do that."

He put the card on the wrought iron coffee table between us, patting it before he released it. He straightened up and moved to the double screen doors opening onto the back yard. He was quiet, his back to us.

"Is that all?" I asked impatiently. "Is that really all you have to say? Just that she liked to *wander*?" Tolly squeezed my hand as if to silence me. I looked him in the face and said, "Don't! I deserve more."

Daddy wouldn't be pushed. In his own good time, he turned around and said, "There were responsibilities. I'm not sorry that I—. No, that's not quite the truth. I am sorry," he continued. "I'm sorry for a lot of things, just not for that. I couldn't just pick up to go gallivanting across the country with a young child and no means of support. It may have been the sixties, but that world of craziness was somewhere beyond Caulfield.

"It was ludicrous to think I could exchange that kind of gypsy existence for what I knew was safe and real. And Gran, I couldn't abandon her. Should I have told you this? Maybe. But I couldn't think how to dress it up so it would make any sense and not break your heart even worse. Maybe it all goes back to her being locked up in that orphanage and needing to feel free. All I know is that she just wanted to be someplace different every day. And she was willing to pay the price. That's what I've never come to terms with. We were the price, Christie. You and I were the price."

My tears stopped. Who knew what poor Tolly must be thinking, me weeping for hours and my normally quiet father, speaking more words at one time than we had ever heard. Tolly continued to hold my hand, more gently now.

Daddy and I watched each other as it all soaked in. He looked sad. For the first time, I felt truly sorry for him. He still loves my mother, I thought.

"So why today, Daddy? Why did she come today?" I said it

softly, hoping to convey my change of spirit. I wanted him to know I had finally uncurled my fists.

"Oh, I don't think she did, honey. I think that was probably her sister, who's kept your mama's secrets and rescued her for years. I could be wrong, but that's where I'd put my money."

I had listened and heard and it was just as I thought. It *had* been something larger that took her away. There was something else I knew for sure. That *was* my mama in the bank. I knew it to the soles of my feet and no one, not even my daddy, who was a far better man than I had ever realized, could take that away. Mama might still be restless, but she had finally decided to wander home. She needed to have that one last look, to be reminded of what she was leaving behind.

Cooking for Two

In May of 1952, my mother sat me down a month before my wedding to give me that obligatory talk, the dreaded one in which she would cover in the shortest amount of time possible, all those important things she thought I was required to know before setting off into the sunset with my true love. With that in mind, Mama came at me broadside late one night just after Bill had dropped me at home and I was feeling all soft and dreamy from our goodnight kisses.

After the questions about where we had gone, and who all we had run into, and whether or not the movie was worth seeing, and had we stopped to have a vanilla shake, she followed me to my room and took a seat on the extra twin bed. Instinctively, I knew what was coming when she cleared her throat and began, "Now Jeanie, dear . . ."

I thought that if I held my breath and bit my tongue it would soon be over, and perhaps I could get through without shuddering or giving up a hysterical giggle. I decided not to look at Mama directly unless it seemed absolutely necessary.

I began to pass the longest twenty minutes of my life by examining the wallpaper, concentrating on the repeat pattern of honeysuckle and lilies of the valley. All the while she talked, fingering the blue candlewicking on the spread with her left hand. I sat on the other bed making little noises of assent, nodding my head when it seemed appropriate and twisting my engagement ring until she reached across the divide and put her hand on mine.

"There's nothing to be embarrassed about, dear. It's just a part of being married. You'll get used to things and know just exactly how to do what's required. You must trust me on this."

I had done my best not to hear her, listening instead to the chatter in my head, which basically consisted of singing "Jesus loves me, this I know" and counting from one to a hundred over and over. When she took my hand and spoke so directly, I had an overwhelming urge to either faint or run. Instead, being the daughter she expected me to be, I feigned a blush and said, "Yes ma'am. Could we please call it a night? I'm very tired."

I came away from that chat with two small details that stuck in my mind; one because it was so horrifyingly personal and the other because I have since found it to be true. First, a vinegar douche does *not* prevent pregnancy. And second, the hardest thing in married life is to learn how to cook for two. There's a natural tendency to fix too much.

I had a friend who never learned the knack of buying food by the ounce or pound. She counted pieces, buying things in numbers, like seventeen green beans: twelve for her hungry husband and five for herself. It seemed to work well and she rarely had leftovers. I, on the other hand, have always had difficulty making a meal turn out just right. My husband, and later my family of four, suffered through many a meal of leftovers. My tendency to prepare too much food has been appreciated at Thanksgiving and Christmas, if not so much in between. I was always given the job of making the dressing and corn pudding, the two family favorites, thus assuring there would be leftovers for everyone to take home.

That's all changed. There are just the three of us here in town now.

My difficult father will be ninety-two this year. He's just been moved into an extended care facility. He's feeble and his memory is failing. He hardly notices what he eats. Mama, who just turned ninety but doesn't look a day over seventy-five, is still in our family home, taking care of the house and yard. Twice a day, she drives back and forth to see Daddy.

Both of my girls are married with children of their own and have long since moved away. They usually visit in the summers, rarely during the holidays.

Bill, who stayed and loved me for some fifty years, developed late-onset diabetes and died of complications this past January. Nothing will ever be the same.

Mama stopped by just before lunch one day last week. She came bearing a pink Tupperware bowl of curried chicken over basmati rice. She set it down on the kitchen table almost reluctantly and stood there making circles on the lid with her forefinger. I watched her and waited. When she looked up at me, her eyes were shiny.

"What's wrong, Mama? What's going on?"

She lowered her head as she cleared her throat and began to speak slowly and so softly I had to strain to hear.

"Jeanie," she began, "I was wrong about a lot of things and I'm sorry if I misled you. I never meant to. Please believe me when I say it wasn't deliberate."

"Misled me? About what? Whatever it is, it surely can't be worth crying over, Mama." I reached for her hand and waited. She lifted her face and looked at me openly.

"Honey, you should know it's *not* true that there's enough time to do everything you want to do in this life. And it's *not* true that the worst kinds of people will necessarily change if you're kind and understanding and give them time. Not always. Not even with prayer."

"I know, Mama," I said. "I've learned that on my own. Don't *worry* yourself about such stuff." I gave her hand a little squeeze.

"And Jeanie," she said, "the hardest thing in married life is *not* learning to cook for two. It's having to learn to cook for one. But then, I guess you already know that, don't you?"

Palmetto Dreams

The town of Palmetto Grove lies inland and is bordered on two sides by counties that touch big water, one the Gulf of Mexico, the other the Atlantic. Going there to visit my grandparents when I was young, no one considered that this flat, gray-sand place would one day be prime real estate because of its proximity to the beaches. Then, it was just a cozy little farming community, one store with a single gas pump connected to the post office and a slightly larger, but still one-room grocery up on the two-lane concrete highway. Going to the beaches was something we never considered. It was the local springs, cool and clear and deep, that held our interest from the first of May through Labor Day.

My grandparents were country people. Granddaddy was a retired stationmaster for Seaboard Air Line Railroad and my grandmother kept house. No help, none asked for, none volunteered.

Granddaddy's big outing each day was going to the post office mid-morning and to the depot to visit and to see if the train was running on schedule. When the timing was right, he'd let me help him swing the long hook with the mail bag onto the morning train as it idled on the track, heading south to Tampa and Palm Beach. Beyond that, he mostly just sat.

Nice days, he sat on the porch in the south swing, shielded by the morning glory-covered lattice. When he wasn't napping, he was whistling and mumbling ancient ditties as he spit tobacco juice into the front hedge.

> *"Jay bird sittin' on a*
> *hickory limb*
> > *He winked at me and I*
> *winked at him"*

Early of a morning, he would sit in the front room in the old brown, cracked-leather rocker, one hand cupping his ear to better hear the radio. On a good weather day, his tobacco juice went out the side window into the coral vine that caught the pungent brown spittle when he lifted the screen. Other times, he used the Maxwell House can resting on the floor by his chair.

While Granddaddy sat and listened and chewed a plug he cut from a tobacco bar he "hid" in the bottom drawer of the chifforobe, Grandmama was hard at work from before dawn till after dark. She cooked three full meals on a wood-burning stove in a kitchen the size of a large storage closet, tossing her dishwater onto the hydrangea bushes beneath the one window by the sink. Every morning, she turned and fluffed their heavy feather mattress as she began her day. When the weather was cold, she was up earlier than usual, lighting fires in the wood-burning stoves. She was the one to ring the chickens' necks, to plunge them into the scalding pot out back that was also used to boil clothes and make soap. She was the one who sat on the rawhide stool in the kitchen, churning butter and pulling off the buttermilk to go with the cornbread for my granddaddy's lunch. In between times, she worked the sewing machine treadle with speed, making feed sack pinafores and navy and white sailor dresses for me, and an occasional Sunday dress for herself.

When I went to stay, Grandmama did everything she could think of to please me and keep me entertained. She found time to take me to visit her neighbors to show me off, and the ladies would reciprocate, bringing their daughters and nieces to call on Sunday afternoons. She made trays of vanilla ice in the old refrigerator topped with coils wound like an old lady's bun. Each afternoon, I was served my favorite snack of cold pork and beans with bread and butter and Vienna sausages. She baked vanilla sponge cake and my most favorite, butterscotch pudding made from scratch.

Grandmama sat with me on the concrete front steps playing games that were surely designed for more than just the two of us. She rarely fussed at me, even when I banged on the out-of-tune piano for hours on end and twirled the kittens by their front legs until they got dizzy and fell over.

In the middle of January when I was five, my mother went into confinement with her pregnancy and I was shipped off to Palmetto Grove. Grandmama moved to the middle bedroom where she and I slept together in an old iron bed. Every night, we lay in the dark, listening for the night train, talking and talking about the baby. I wanted a girl, a baby sister to play with. It was the last thing we talked about at night and the first thing every morning. Grandmama would prop up, her waist-length hair down from its braid, spreading a yellowed white veil across the goose feather pillows. She listened to me chatter, patiently answering the same questions over and over. Why was it taking so long, when would she come, how long before I could see her, was she sure my mama was all right, what would the baby look like?

February was damp and raw. I had a nasty cold and my eyes were infected. I had to stay in. Every morning, I waited hopefully as Granddaddy went out for his post office run. News came at the end of the first week. Grandmama read and reread Daddy's letter. I had my baby sister. We talked about how little she must be, with blue eyes, different from mine. Mama had to stay in the hospital for ten days then get settled at home. It seemed forever before Daddy would come to get me. Grandmama showed me a calendar and we counted off the days.

One morning as I trailed along behind her, I tripped on my dangling shoelace and fell against the hot wood stove in the bedroom. The left side of my face and my left arm were badly burned. Grandmama coated my blistered skin with Unguentine, a smelly yellow petroleum salve which held the heat and prolonged the healing process, and wrapped me in rolled gauze. It was standard treatment for burns. It was also the worst thing she could have done. The pain was terrible.

Granddaddy took up his black ink pen and wrote in his telegraphic script on a lined sheet of tablet paper to tell my folks about the accident. It was 1942 and there was gas rationing, but somehow Daddy worked it out. He left Mama and the baby to drive four hours south to check on me. Later on, he told Mama that when he walked in and saw me curled up in Grandmama's arms in the rocker, it broke his heart. I was swathed in bandages, with a runny nose and pinkeye, and because I couldn't bathe, my hair hadn't been washed in days.

He arrived early one morning and put me in the car to drive ten miles to see a druggist, someone he had grown up with. The man prescribed drops for the pinkeye and Vicks for my runny nose. Back at the house, Daddy cut my hair with sewing shears then leaned me backward into the kitchen sink to shampoo the matted mess. The fear and distress he must have felt turned to anger. It showed in his pinched mouth, in the way he gripped my arm, in his tight voice. Forever after, I remembered that look and learned to see it as a clear signal that I was in trouble.

Because he loved and respected his mama, Daddy could not upbraid her for the condition I was in, so it fell to me to catch the blame for all that was wrong. Someone had to be at fault . . . for the fall, for the nasty cold, for the pinkeye, and the dirty hair. *I'd been careless, he said, should have been watching what I was doing. Had no business being so close to that stove. Shouldn't have been talking. Couldn't I keep my shoes tied? I'd been warned again and again. See what had happened? Now I couldn't go home to Mama and the baby. Not for weeks. Not until I was completely well.*

I understood the punishment. I just didn't understand why. How had catching my shoelace on the loose corner of the metal protector underneath the stove caused it all, not just the burns, but the nasty cough, the runny nose, my mattering eyes? It was always this way with Daddy. I never knew when the blame would come or why.

He stayed for the day and one night and then he was gone, back to Mama and my baby sister. I cried when he drove away. I was hurt and sick and I had been punished and deserted. Grandmama took me to the kitchen to sit with her while she made me pudding.

A few days later, I received a large, heavy box through the mail. I was excited. Games most likely, or maybe a doll. But it was filled with big cans of orange and pineapple juice. They would heal me, Daddy wrote. The orange juice tasted of tin and the pineapple juice was so sweet I gagged. Grandmama insisted I finish every drop so that she could write Daddy a good report. He had frightened her too, I think.

Of course, I recovered from all of it in time; the cough, the cold, the pinkeye and the burns, despite the Unguentine and tinny-tasting fruit juice. The scars were not permanent and eventually faded to nothing.

Finally, in mid-March, I got to go home. I was happy to see Mama and my pretty baby girl. But she was so tiny. "How long before she's big enough to play?" I asked.

It's been seventy-plus years since that winter and I still have dreams about Palmetto Grove. I yearn for those days in that long lost town, going to the post office and the depot with Granddaddy. Fascinated by his ability to accurately spit tobacco from a distance into the station's brass spittoon, I miss those outings and the times he sat with me on the swing and taught me nonsensical rhymes. I miss going to the store on the way to Cross Creek where he took me for what I called "pink pillow" suckers and a beer for himself.

I long to have Grandmama sew for me again and take me to visit, to play stoop games in the afternoon and let me plunder through her button box, to sooth me with a backrub or a bowl of pudding. I want to see her long hair come down from its pins and watch her rinse it in rainwater caught under the back eves in an old wooden barrel. I want to do it all again.

But time passes and things change. Life gets complicated and bad things happen. And now, especially now, my heart aches for the time when Grandmama told me my prayers had been answered, that I had my new baby sister, the one who came along to be my playmate and most loyal friend, who showed me love in a million ways, and who, when no more drugs could ease her pain and no amount of praying make her well, died last spring and left me far too soon. It seems our time together had barely begun.

And now, when I truly need it most, I find there is no comfort to be found in a bowl of butterscotch pudding—not even one made from scratch.

A Parting Gift

On Valentine's Day, when we came to visit, Daddy told us that Mama had been in a deep sleep all day. I didn't understand why he hadn't called for help, or an ambulance. He seemed muddled himself, so I didn't push it.

As we gathered around their bed, he attempted to wake her. When roused, she was confused, frighteningly disoriented. At first, she peered at us as if we were intruders. The angry-sounding words she sputtered made no sense, but hurt me nonetheless. When our parents lose their mental capabilities and quite obviously have no control, there is still that doubt that creeps in, and we, the watching children, wonder if perhaps they really do know, if perhaps they are at last showing the truth about how they feel, have always felt, about us. My kind mother, who always strived to please, was nowhere to be seen. We were entering an unknown realm and I was scared.

Although she softened when she saw my daughter and her girls, she didn't fully understand the heart-shaped balloons or cards we offered. She seemed to question our intentions. Gestures of love, of caring, seemed unwelcome. Within hours, she slipped into her first coma.

In the hospital, after a dietary change that temporarily revived her failing liver, she appeared to have physically recovered. For several days, it seemed that her physician's dire predictions were unwarranted. She watched reruns of *Matlock* on TV when I visited in the evenings, barely taking notice of me, acting as if there was no reason for my company.

She was proud of her recent manicure and her nails. She held up her hands and admired them—her polished nails, the longest they had ever been. Propped up in bed, makeup on, hair neatly combed, she looked like her old self.

During this awful week, my sister's boy, her only child, was killed in an automobile accident. Divorced and living alone, my sister was coping as best she could with the help of her son's friends. She did not want a service of any kind. Her son would be cremated and she and his father would scatter the ashes in the woods where their son had loved to hunt.

I offered to tell Mama. My sister believed Mama would react to such news as she might have in the past, with lots of tears and concern for my sister in particular. She would want to be taken to her immediately. But *this* Mama responded as if I were speaking of someone she barely knew. She spoke her grandson's name and said, "Oh . . . that's too bad." Looking straight ahead, she never took her eyes off Andy Griffith.

When I inquired as I got ready to leave, she said, no, she didn't need anything, and no, she didn't want anything—except pizza. She wanted me to bring her a pepperoni pizza. I said that I would, but after thinking it over, I never did. Her doctor had said no protein, no salt, no fat. But in the end, what difference would it have made? She was a prisoner, albeit of her failing body, requesting her last meal. And I refused her. What sort of person breaks a promise and refuses her dying mother's final request? One who is terrified, afraid of participating in any action, no matter how small, that might hasten her mother's death.

Amazingly, Mama went home once more for a short time. Daddy dressed her each morning and led her to the living room where she sat near him in a matching recliner, silently watching and waiting for the weather to change.

I wonder if she knew it would be her last time to sit, staring out the window beside her chair, looking to the world beyond the tiny rose garden Daddy had planted for her, just in her line of vision. She was waiting for spring to come before she gave it up for good.

But it was gray and cold, an ugly beginning to March. Nothing was in bloom, certainly not the favored red Mr. Lincoln roses. I fastened a plastic butterfly on a suction cup to a window pane. She never acknowledged it, although it was always within her view. Day by day, she continued to withdraw further and further into herself. Mama was fading, disappearing before us, and there was nothing I could do. I, too, waited—waited for my shy sweet mother with the gentle disposition to return. But she had gone, as surely as if she had walked out the door with no backward glance. She had left me forever.

Drifting into another coma before the week was out, she was back in the hospital. Her final rally was for a few short hours before she slipped away again. I was not there. I was two hours from home on business. I got the call while standing with my daughter in an antiques shop where we had stopped on our way home. I was holding a small Victorian bisque china flower holder with its original blue ribbon that I had just bought. I planned to fill it with flowers to hang by Mama's bed. Now it was too late. "It could be any time," the doctor said. The phone was steady in my hand, but my insides trembled.

In her room late in the evening, we stood together, my father, my sister, my youngest son, and I, and waited. My father and sister were in denial. In his kindest, sweetest voice Daddy pleaded with Mama to respond. His desperation was difficult to watch. Then he was convinced she was acknowledging him. "Looky, Mama, we're all here." He named each of us. To no one in particular he said, "See how bright those pretty brown eyes are? Mama, I see you trying to smile."

My grieving sister, who stood at his side, was his echo, "Yes,

Mama, I see you smiling!"

My son was young, just twenty-two, and this was his first death watch. He felt it his duty to be there, but it was hard for him. He was quiet, fidgety, and left the room more than once. It was up to me to stay calm, to take charge if need be. We were each suffering our own kind of shock.

The doctor stopped in for a minute and declared there was nothing to explain why Mama continued to breathe. Still, she would not let go.

Sometime after eleven, it came to me what must be done. As Mama struggled, somehow I knew what it was she wanted, what she needed. This time, I would not refuse her. There were different words to be spoken now, difficult words my father could never consider. I did not ask permission, simply took her small, cool hand in mine and began to speak.

"It's okay, Mama. You've been *such* a good girl and done your very best and we're so proud of you. You've fought long and hard. We love you so much and we'll miss you always, Mama, but you're tired and need to rest. Don't worry about Daddy. We'll take care of him. I promise."

Having always tried to be the good little girl, the responsible mother, the best wife, and having been unsure of herself for a lifetime, Mama had needed reassurance . . . and permission to take her leave. My words were hardly spoken when away she flew.

$\backsim$

Within the week, the sun broke through. Shortly after, the earth warmed, trees began to bud and spring came to stay. Angry, I cried. Why now, I railed, why not a few short days ago? All Mama wanted was to see the world in bloom one last time.

"Yes," someone said, seeking to console, "but think of this: your mother is now in a place where there's eternal spring." It sounded platitudinous. I wasn't so sure.

Better than that, I liked it when some kind soul suggested that it was Mama herself who had coaxed forth our bashful spring, a parting gift to comfort those she loved.

On a fine day in June, when the deep red Mr. Lincolns bloomed on the bush my daddy had planted, I picked two of the prettiest roses. One I took to the cemetery to lay like a prayer on Mama's stone marker. The other I placed in the Victorian bisque flower holder that hangs at the foot of my bed.

SECOND CHANCE

I've come home from Atlanta to spend a few days for my twin sisters' high school graduation. They're the last of us five kids to finish and that is a good enough reason for a visit. I've stayed away for nearly two years and have run out of excuses. It's reminders of the hard life we led here and that my mother continues to live that have kept me from coming back.

I'm the first on either side of the family to go to college. I worked at Sampson's Drugs during high school then got a partial scholarship to the community college. Daddy fought me about going. He wanted me working full time, bringing in money, but my need for learning was stronger than his objections.

I worked in the school library while I got my AA. I wanted—still want—to finish college, but I had to get away from home or die. I got hired by an insurance company in Atlanta, so off I went. No regrets about leaving. I'm hoping to convince my sisters to do something beyond this life here. They have boyfriends and seem content working at Kroger's, but I want more for them.

Driving the three hours home on Friday put knots in my stomach. Pulling up to the house brought on that familiar feeling of fear and nausea. The fear is that I might somehow get caught here and be unable to escape. I firmly believe I was born into this family through some cosmic error. It's as plain as the nose on my freckled face that I don't belong. Nausea is my way of dealing with anything unpleasant. I stay nauseated a lot.

Mama grew up on a dirt farm in the South Georgia backwoods where her daddy did his best to grow corn and peanuts to keep her and her eleven siblings from starving during a time when the whole country had gone to pot and was next to death. My graduating twin sisters, Mary Catherine and Marie, were named for Catholic nuns who taught Mama and three of her sisters when they were sent off to "visit" an orphanage until such time as there was space and money enough to keep them at home again.

Granddaddy Tomkins' crops had failed and it was nearly four years before the girls were reunited with their family. When they were allowed to return home, my mother, Elva, cried and began the habit of gnawing her fingernails which continues to this day. Having become accustomed to the loving care at the orphanage, she didn't want to go back to sleeping three in a bed on the front screen porch where passersby could see their poverty up close.

On this first visit I've made home since my escape from what I believed to be Hell itself, I think I can, for the first time, accurately see Mama as others—my friends, strangers—must have seen her forever: a ruddy, moon-faced, country woman with thin, lank hair held back from her sun-blotched face with a child's pink and blue plastic hairclips. I believe they are teddy bears, their features nearly rubbed off by wear. How I viewed her before is unclear. It's almost as if I didn't see her at all. I find that disturbing.

This Monday morning, we sit in Dr. Hawkins' waiting room with its slightly off-balance ceiling fan squeaking away as it stirs the muggy air on this early June day.

Even at nine-fifteen, the room is almost full so that Mama and I have to sit in the last vacant chairs at either side of the room. I glance at her from over the ratty, three-year-old *Family Circle* I find in my chair. She's sitting very still, staring into space at nothing in particular. I know she can sit this way for hours, never changing expression unless someone comes in, when she will acknowledge them with a slight nod and a weak smile.

She's dressed in what is commonly called a house dress. It serves Mama as her best. The pink-flowered cotton, faded by many washings and finely starched, has little white buttons down the bodice. Mama's a good thirty or forty pounds too heavy which causes the buttons to pull and her patent leather belt to roll under at the waist.

Her only jewelry, a silver sliver of a band on her left hand, is obscured by a puffy knuckle. Her nails are bitten to the quick. Both hands clutch a worn black patent purse which she holds on her lap, poised it would seem, to protect valuables. I turn away and pretend to be engrossed in the only picture hanging, a country scene with a man leaning against a fence, staring off into the surrounding wheat fields and the distant purple-topped mountains. She is not my idea of what a mother should look like, how she should dress, how she should be. I'm embarrassed to be seen with her which makes me angry with myself.

I agreed to come with her to Dr. Hawkins', though I'm not sure what the visit is for. A checkup, I suppose. I didn't ask. I'm familiar with the office which has changed little over the years. All of my family have come here at one time or other. Once, when three of us children had mumps at the same time, the doctor came to us. I doubt he still makes house calls. He's into his late sixties and has been practicing for thirty-five years.

When Mama was barely seventeen, she left home to marry John Talton. He was nineteen, the only child of a local bricklayer whose wife had died early. They moved in with Mr. Talton to keep him company. John was set to take up his daddy's trade, but was killed when he fell backwards off a scaffold while working on the new City Bank thirty miles away. He and Mama had been married just three months. She was already pregnant.

Mr. Talton offered to let Mama stay on after John's death, but her folks dug in their heels and insisted she "come on back home where you belong at a time like this." Whether caused by the shock of her new husband's death or the shock of being wrenched back into her family's bosom, the boy baby came two months early. He was buried next to John and Mrs. Talton at the New Canaan Baptist Church Cemetery on the back road to Pelham.

When she can get a ride, Mama still goes out there to tend the graves and lay flowering branches out on the ground in front of the markers. Sometimes she puts out wildflowers in a quart jar full of rainwater with a teaspoon of sugar to help hold the blossoms. From the time I was old enough to walk, she would take me with her.

By nine forty-five, the room has turned over once and refilled, including three coughing children and a mother holding a fretting, feverish two-year-old who won't be comforted. He's too sick to be put on the floor where he wants to be and too restless to sit still without fussing. I wish I was anywhere but here.

Eventually, Mrs. Quick, who has been Dr. Hawkins' nurse forever, calls Mama in for her turn. Here it's always first come, no appointment necessary. Mama rises slowly and I notice that her ankles are puffed above her shoe tops, like lumps of rising dough. It's obvious now that something is "bad wrong" as my granny would have said. The nausea's back, along with a clutching in my chest.

I grow irritated watching the young mother struggle with the fussing baby. No one else seems to be bothered. I walk outside for a breath of air. It's going to be another fine day except for the humidity which is already causing the mossy trees to drip.

A man drives by and honks, throwing up a hand in my direction. I have no idea who he might be. Could be somebody who knows me or could just be that sign of friendly recognition still practiced around here. It's a small town in a rural county where old-time courtesies still exist. I wave and go back inside to wait with the other restless children.

The door opens behind me and, instinctively, I know what's coming next. "Enid? Dr. Hawkins wants to see you." Mrs. Quick holds the door for me. "Come on back. Your mama's gettin' dressed." I let out an audible sigh which causes the baby's mother to glance in my direction.

"Well, Enid," Dr. Hawkins greets me, "it's nice to have you home."

I'm surprised to see he's aged so well. Still a handsome man, just a bit grayer. He's wearing a signet ring of some kind, his fingers long, like a concert pianist. I wonder why he's never married.

"I know you must be worried about your mother. Glad you made her come in when you did." He studies her chart.

I think I might faint and realize I haven't answered Dr. Hawkins. I'm standing in the middle of his tiny, windowless office, hoping for the world to stop spinning as I try to stutter a response.

"Yes, sir, well I didn't realize there was anything wrong, but I guess that's no excuse and I—. Could I please sit down, Dr. Hawkins? I don't feel so well. It's hot and I—"

He ignores my attempt to justify ignorance and steps right over my words, motioning me to a two-seater couch where I plop down with a jolt that jerks my neck.

"I'll speak to her again before you leave, but I know you'll be the one to make the arrangements." In that terrifying split second before he continues, my confusion leads me to believe he means funeral arrangements. My heart has stopped beating, but it hiccups and catches speed as he goes on to say, "I'll get Mrs. Quick to call ahead, but you need to make sure you get your mama to the hospital this afternoon."

He looks up at me and I nod compliantly, "Yes, sir." I never realized his eyes were so blue.

"Go have your lunch and pack her a few things for the next couple of days. Then get yourself on out there as soon as you can. I make rounds at four and I'll want to see her then. I'll get the tests ordered . . . and they're quick about getting things back to me. But even so, she'll be there at least a day or two. We've got to get that swelling under control. I'll know better by this time tomorrow where we're headed."

He stands and walks toward the door which is my signal to leave. "Any questions? Tell your daddy not to worry. The bill is something we can talk about later."

He calls for Mrs. Quick and I move out into the waiting room where the hot, feverish baby is now crawling around on the floor. The mother has apparently given up. The other children are calling to him as if he is a pet, a kitten or puppy they hope will crawl in their direction.

Mama comes out from the examining room. "I guess you talked to Dr. Hawkins. I'm sorry to be such a trouble."

"No, Mama, it's no trouble. I wish I'd known you needed me. I just want to get you well." I am surprised by my words which express new, real concern. I bite my lip not to cry.

When I reach for her, my fingers make a print on her swollen arm. I pull back.

I walk ahead to the car and for the first time in my life I open the door for her. As she settles into her seat, she looks up at me and smiles. I see that her eyes are hooded from the fluid collecting in her face.

I'm thankful beyond thankful that no one is at home on this Monday noon. The twins left late Friday night after graduation and are off on their very first house party, up on Lake Alatoona. My brothers are working a sawmill down in Sneads with an uncle. Daddy is where he always is, up to no good, I'm sure. I don't think I could face him right now without letting loose a world of anger.

I know my father was once a good and dependable man because Mama and her family have all said so. There is a small silver, wood frame on their bureau that holds a picture of them as newlyweds. They're standing on the steps of the courthouse where they were married about nine months after Mama buried her baby. Daddy has his arm around Mama's shoulders and is smiling a great broad smile. He's in a dark suit with a straw hat in his hand, his hair slicked back. Mama, thin and looking for all the world like one of the pretty twins, is in a pale cotton dress, holding a single rose. I search for her smile, but it seems more a look of resignation.

I know she'll want this picture with her so I lay it on top of her housecoat and underwear and snap the catch on the suitcase I've packed. If I had my way, I'd put her few things in a paper sack. Knowing that would surely embarrass her, I use the musty old suitcase that is large and awkward to carry.

We get to Dawson County Hospital about one-thirty and find that Mrs. Quick has made the promised arrangements. I'm left with little to do but sign a few papers. The staff is pleasant and efficient. Mama's in a hospital gown with a thermometer in her mouth before I can get her unpacked. After the aide leaves us, Mama smooths back her sheets. I crank up the bed so she has a better view of the TV.

"I hadn't been in the hospital since the twins," she says. "I didn't know they'd got air conditioning. This is real nice. I like this green color on the wall. I thought ever'thing had to be white so's they could tell when it gets dirty." She looks around the room approvingly. "They've got to have it sanitary," she adds.

I find us a game show to watch and settle into one of those low, badly engineered hospital visitor's chairs that throws your body backwards into a 30-degree angle, making it impossible to sit up straight.

I close my eyes to rest and jump with a start when someone wins a complete dinette set and the studio audience goes wild. Mama has dozed off also. I make it up out of the ridiculous chair and turn down the volume. I sneak out of the room so as not to disturb her nap and go to find a snack. Or a meal. I eat in times of stress.

The small cafeteria is clean and white, which may very well have something to do with Mama's color theory. I can smell cooking that could be lunch or might be the early dinner. Either way, I've gotten here too late or too soon for the single-line buffet.

A machine gives me a choice of three kinds of cold sandwiches. I choose pimiento cheese and am assured by the label that it is made with mayonnaise, not salad dressing. That's important. I have chips, a slice of chocolate cake and a Coke which I take outside to a concrete bench by the front door. I'm reminded of a car picnic on the way to Granny's when I was little. Only the deviled eggs are missing. I must remember to tell Mama.

Dr. Hawkins is good to his word and shows up right at four o'clock. I excuse myself while he and the nurse do Mama's second physical of the day. When I come back into the room, he is leaning over the sliding bed table, writing orders for tests and medications.

"I've put your mother on a diuretic and a low salt diet to pull out and limit some of this fluid you see pooling. I'm not going any further with treatment 'til I get some studies back." This is directed at me with a firm scowl. I have the fleeting fear that he holds me responsible in some way for what's going on. I close the door behind him as he leaves and Mama and I wait to see what comes next. Eventually, we hear the clacking food cart being wheeled toward her room.

After Mama finishes her salt-free meal at five-thirty, I set her up with the TV clicker and make certain she knows how to operate the emergency buzzer. I leave to go home and face the music with Daddy . . . if he's there.

I think about my parents on the way to the house. The only reason I know much about Mama's past is because of her sister, Aunt Edna, the talker. She's what's known as a nervous Nellie. She can't seem to keep still or quiet. I had to share my bed with her once when she came to visit and I experienced firsthand that she tosses in her sleep and mumbles through the night. I'm betting that's why her marriage didn't work out.

It was Aunt Edna who told me that Daddy was once a "nice looking, very good man" and that only "hardship of the worst kind" is what changed Joe Hooks. All my life I've heard stories about the mill closing, Mama's depressions, the bad economy, Daddy's hepatitis, and all the rest. I don't know how much is real and how much is offered up as excuse for Daddy's going from job to job, sometimes with long weeks in between. Either way, what I've known is the results. There may not have been money for this household, but there was always money in his pocket for cigarettes and beer. I've heard there were women.

He's in front of the TV when I come in. I didn't much think he'd be home this early. He looks up and asks about Mama's whereabouts. "There's no supper started and she's gone off without so much as a fiddley-damn-dee."

I want to slap him. Instead I take a deep breath. "In the hospital, Daddy. She's gone to the hospital. She's sick, real sick." I'm angry enough that I don't care to break it to him gently. I say it this way to shock him . . . like that might cause him to instantly change his ways.

He sits there, blinking at me with those pale blue, peeled-grape eyes. He is stunned.

Finally, "Wha' do you mean, sick? She was fine this mornin' when I left!"

There it is. *Another* accusation to fuel my guilt.

"No, sir, she wasn't fine. She hasn't been fine for a long time. You should've taken more notice of her. I hope for all our sakes it isn't too late!" I add this last for effect.

I walk over and turn off the TV and take a stand by the door to the kitchen. I believe I can hear Daddy's brain churning. I cross my arms and wait.

"Well, damn it, Enie, are you gonna tell me or not? What the hell's wrong with your mama?"

That's more like it, I think. I'm glad to see you're scared.

I take a seat on the worn, moss-colored velvet couch, and tell him what I know. He watches me with those pale, watery eyes, smoking, smoking, not saying a word until I've finished. He puts out his cigarette, says he's going to see her and goes off to get a bath. Twenty minutes later, he's gone.

I hear him come back a little after nine and go straight to bed. I've already curled up to try to get some rest myself. I crawl under the covers and begin to count backward from a hundred.

I wake around six-thirty to the smell of coffee and toast. Daddy doesn't know me well enough to know I don't drink caffeine or eat anything but cereal for breakfast. No matter. It's a nice gesture and he's up and doing.

"Gonna check on your mama before I get to work," he says from my doorway. "Doc's got her anxious about them tests. There's coffee made." I nod and he's gone.

Mornings in any hospital are pretty much the same. They wake you early to see how you've slept, chatter in the hallways clanging trays and bedpans and metal carts, and swing in and out of patient rooms with mops and pails and lots of questions. I go in at ten, hoping to miss the fuss. Sure enough, Mama has seen the doctor, had a shower, and her bed has been changed. They've already drawn blood for tests, but that doesn't stop them from drawing more. Just after lunch, they come to take her for kidney tests. It's after three when they get her back to bed. I must remember to bring a book. I can watch just so much of this local TV.

It's after four when I hear Dr. Hawkins in the hall talking to the duty nurse. The door swings open and he takes a seat on the edge of Mama's bed. Here it comes.

"It's not so simple, Mrs. Hooks. You've got a lot goin' on. But I can tell you this: you're gonna feel much better in a few days, and if you work with me, you're gonna be a different woman. That should be some good news."

My reaction is mixed. Tell us something specific, please.

As if on cue, he continues, "Mrs. Hooks, you've got high blood pressure and diabetes we need to get under control so you don't end up with kidney involvement or heart problems. We can do that with diet and medication for now. When you're feelin' better, I want you to start walking every day. This is nothin' to play around with so I need you to follow my instructions. Okay?" Mama nods penitently.

"I'll see you again in the morning. Maybe we can let you go on Friday . . . depends on your sugar levels. In the bathroom a lot last night, I bet." Mama nods again. "That's good. We need to get rid of that dangerous fluid. Keep it up."

As he heads toward the door, he turns and looks at me. "You're lucky this daughter of yours cared enough to get you in when she did. Good to see you again, Enid." My breath catches. And then he's gone.

Trying to take it all in, I want to run after him and ask questions, get more answers. I want him to listen to me, to understand that I *didn't* know, didn't have a thing to do with Mama getting to his office when she did. I am most definitely *not* the daughter he thinks I am. He needs to know.

Sure enough, as Dr. Hawkins predicted, by Friday, Mama is looking and feeling better overall and is ready to be released. I take all her paperwork in hand and walk beside her to the car while an orderly pushes her in a wheelchair. As we drive away, I see her looking back almost wistfully.

We drop off her prescriptions at Sampson's and I take her home for a nap. The phone rings as we walk in. It's my brother Wilson, calling to check in. I called my brothers after Dr. Hawkins gave us a diagnosis. Mama seems happy to hear from Wil and sends her love to Tommy. She takes to her bed and closes her eyes for a rest.

During this week, Daddy's been showing signs of what he must have been at one time before "hardship of the worst kind" befell him. He went to see Mama twice every day in the hospital and is home on this Friday night by six-thirty. From the looks of him, it's clear he's been working somewhere. He's uttered no complaints and said not a single word about the bills. Hallelujah, praise Jesus!

I drive downtown to pick up the prescriptions and stop by Joey's to get a pizza for Daddy and me and a salad for Mama. We're all whipped and ready to turn in early.

Saturday morning is a June day at its best: sunny with high clouds, only slightly hazy early, not much humidity. It's a perfect day and I have a plan.

Mama agrees to come with me. I help her into the car and we take off to the local strip mall. It wouldn't be my first choice, but this is not Atlanta. Surely someone here at Cut-N-Curl can do a simple cut and shampoo. It seems that Lorene is available right now and will be glad to help us. When Lorene has her situated, Mama leans back into the shampoo bowl and a little smile turns the corners of her mouth.

Forty-five minutes later, Mama, Lorene, and I stare into the mirror over Lorene's station. "It's simple and real easy for her to take care of," Lorene says to me as if referring to my child. "I'm sure glad you let me tweeze them brows!"

"Well, Mama, what do you think? I think it makes you look ten years younger."

It's true. Lorene has shortened and layered Mama's hair to take advantage of her natural wave. She finished with an auburn rinse that adds a depth of color and shine to Mama's otherwise drab brown hair.

Lorene gives Mama a hand mirror and swivels her chair so she can take a look at the back. Mama turns her head one way and then another as she studies her reflection in the mirror over Lorene's station. "It's real nice, Enie. I like it a lot, Miss Lorene. I wonder what your daddy will say."

Mama reaches to the counter and picks up her hairclips. The faceless teddy bears slip into her purse for safekeeping.

We each get a salad at Eileen's Bakery and Sandwich Shop and head to Belk's where I help Mama choose two new outfits, one for every day and one for good. (I will not mention shoes until the swelling in her feet goes away.) Anything more and Mama would cease to be willing and happy. She can handle just so much good fortune.

We wander through Kroger's and pick out fruit for her to have between meals. I buy bottles of spring water to have on hand. Back in the car, at my insistence, she eats an apple and drinks a bottle of the water. It's the first store-bought water she's ever had, she says.

When we get home, we settle down for a nap, tired from the trauma of the week and the measured excitement of the morning. Daddy's off working somewhere.

About six o'clock, he comes in looking like someone who's had a rough day in the heat. He's been helping out at Joe Barwick's auto shop, he says. I can only imagine how hot it gets in that corrugated metal building with no air. He doesn't complain and stops to check on Mama before he cleans up.

After his bath, he and I sit for a while on the front steps, waiting for the world to cool down before I start supper. The yard needs watering and I see spots where sandspurs have taken over. The house across the street is still vacant and I wonder for how long. Its roof is beginning to rot. A noisy motorbike whizzes by and Daddy frowns.

"Your mama seems real pleased with her new hairdo, Sister. That was a nice thing you did for her today."

"Thank you, Daddy. It's about time I did something good around here." Before he has a chance to respond I jump in again with talk about supper. "I thought I'd fix butter peas and okra and some sliced tomatoes to go with rice and a little pan-fried steak. That okay with you?"

"Sounds good, honey. I'm tired but hungry as a horse."

I've dreaded bringing it up, but the time has come to talk about my leaving. Mama has wandered into the kitchen to sit with me while I cook.

"I'm going to have to get back home, Mama. I'd stay on for the summer if I could," I say, and realize I mean it. "I thought I'd leave tomorrow after lunch sometime."

"I know, girlie." She hasn't called me that in ages. "I can't say enough about your bein' here. I'd been havin' them headaches so bad I couldn't hardly see straight some days and I was worried about all that swellin'. I don't know if I'd 've got up the nerve to get to the doctor by myself if you hadn't of got here. I was thinkin' it might be cancer."

"Oh, Mama," I said. "I'm so sorry. I wish I'd known. Don't you do that again, you hear? We need to take good care of you."

"Well, seems we're on the right track, all right. I'm gettin' better ever' day."

We have supper together and it feels right, the three of us around the table. I call my brothers and they promise to come up on the next weekend to check on things and let me know.

I leave my sisters a letter and ask them to look out for Mama and Daddy and to call me anytime just to talk. I hope they've had a good time on their house party. Being with them that one day was too little, but I was proud to see them walk and get their diplomas on the same football field where I graduated and our brothers played ball.

It's Sunday morning. After breakfast, I sit down with Daddy at the kitchen table. We go over a list of Mama's medications and her diet instructions. He nods compliantly. I suggest he might encourage her to walk a little every day. He says he will.

By two o'clock, we've had a cold lunch and I've said my goodbyes and hugged them both with real feeling. As I drive away, they wave to me from the front walk. In the rearview mirror, I see Daddy reach out to help Mama up the steps and into the house.

I can't say for certain that Mama will keep to her diet and obey Dr. Hawkins' orders any more than I can predict whether Daddy will continue to straighten up and fly right. The odds aren't good on either count. I can't even say with assurance that I'll continue to look on my family with this new, less-jaundiced eye. But for the moment, all is well and I'm content to believe we are having a second chance.

I wonder whether the roses are blooming at the City Park. I'll go by and see. Before I head back home, I think I'll take some out to John and baby boy Talton. It's only a little out of the way.

About Virginia Gwynn...

The author and her devoted dog, Malibu, live in a small Southern town in a Creole-style cottage built in 1848. The dog, the house, and writing are pretty much full-time projects. Family relationships, friends, and food are important in her life and in those of the characters who grace her nostalgic stories. To find out more, go to www.onesouthernvoice.com.

Made in the USA
Charleston, SC
02 July 2014